SECOND ALARM

FIREHOUSE FOURTEEN
BOOK 5

LISA B. KAMPS

Lisa B. Kamps

SECOND ALARM

Firehouse Fourteen
Book 5

Lisa B. Kamps

Lisa B. Kamps

SECOND ALARM

SECOND ALARM
Copyright © 2017 by Elizabeth Belbot Kamps

All rights reserved. Except for use in any review, the reproduction or utilization of this work in whole or in part in any form by any electronic, mechanical or other means, now known or hereafter invented, including xerography, photocopying and recording, or in any information storage or retrieval system, is forbidden without the express written permission of the author.

All characters in this book have no existence outside the imagination of the author and have no relation to anyone bearing the same name or names, living or dead. This book is a work of fiction and any resemblance to any individual, place, business, or event is purely coincidental.

Cover and logo design by Jay Aheer of Simply Defined Art
http://www.simplydefinedart.com/

All rights reserved.
ISBN: 1973826615
ISBN-13: 978-1973826613

DEDICATION

For Dale Winter.
Told you I was going to…

You should know to believe me by now!

SECOND ALARM

Contents

Title Page iii
Copyright vi
Dedication vii
Other titles by this author xi
Chapter One 15
Chapter Two 25
Chapter Three 40
Chapter Four 48
Chapter Five 54
Chapter Six 64
Chapter Seven 73
Chapter Eight 81
Chapter Nine 91
Chapter Ten 102
Chapter Eleven 113
Chapter Twelve 123
Chapter Thirteen 131
Chapter Fourteen 139
Chapter Fifteen 150
Chapter Sixteen 159
Chapter Seventeen 171
Chapter Eighteen 179
Chapter Nineteen 190
Chapter Twenty 198
Chapter Twenty-One 206
Chapter Twenty-Two 212

Chapter Twenty-Three	222
Chapter Twenty-Four	233
Epilogue	241
ABOUT THE AUTHOR	245
CROSSING THE LINE preview	247
PLAYING THE GAME preview	253

Other titles by this author

THE BALTIMORE BANNERS

Crossing The Line, Book 1
Game Over, Book 2
Blue Ribbon Summer, Book 3
Body Check, Book 4
Break Away, Book 5
Playmaker (A Baltimore Banners Intermission novella)
Delay of Game, Book 6
Shoot Out, Book 7
The Baltimore Banners 1st Period Trilogy (Books 1-3)
The Baltimore Banners 2nd Period Trilogy (Books 4-6)
On Thin Ice, Book 8
Coach's Challenge (A Baltimore Banners Intermission Novella)
One-Timer, Book 9
Face Off, Book 10

THE YORK BOMBERS

Playing The Game, Book 1
Playing To Win, Book 2
Playing For Keeps, Book 3
Playing It Up, Book 4

FIREHOUSE FOURTEEN

Once Burned, Book 1
Playing With Fire, Book 2
Breaking Protocol, Book 3
Into The Flames, Book 4

Lisa B. Kamps

Second Alarm, Book 5

STAND-ALONE TITLES

Emeralds and Gold: A Treasury of Irish Short Stories
(anthology)
Finding Dr. Right, Silhouette Special Edition
Time To Heal
Dangerous Passion

SECOND ALARM

Lisa B. Kamps

Chapter One

You don't matter. You never did.

Beth Fuller stood inside the foyer of the restaurant and forced the nagging voice from her mind. Did her hesitation show on her face? Is that why the hostess kept tossing those judging glances her way? Probably. Beth wanted to pretend she didn't notice them; wanted to pretend they didn't matter.

But they did. Oh, how they mattered. They mattered more than she'd ever admit out loud.

You're only good for one thing. Haven't you figured that out yet? And you're not even any good at that!

Had he been right? Was she only good for one thing, one thing she wasn't good at? No, he was wrong. And if he wasn't—so what? She happened to like that one thing. And she happened to miss that one thing— missed it more than she thought she would. Nine months. Nine long, dry months, without even a single prospect.

Was she wrong for coming here tonight? Wrong for wanting a touch, a kiss? Wrong for wanting to *feel*?

Well, too bad. She *did* miss it, and she was tired of waiting for any potential prospects to come to her. It was time to take matters into her own hands.

Well, okay, time to do a little more than that, since her own hand wasn't really cutting it anymore. Not that she had anything against self-gratification—she didn't.

She just wanted *more*.

So she'd done some research and looked into a few online dating sites. Except she didn't want to *date*. Beth had had enough of dating, enough of commitment. She just wanted to have fun. If she'd been a guy, it wouldn't have been an issue—just go to a bar somewhere, strike up a conversation, buy a few drinks, and have her itch taken care of.

Except she wasn't a guy and there were safety considerations to think of—considerations that went beyond safe sex. So picking up some random stranger in a bar was out of the question. At least for her.

Was this really any different?

She pushed the voice—her own, this time—away. Yes, this was different. This wasn't a random pick-up. Not really. She'd chatted some with the guy she was supposed to meet. She'd seen his picture. At least, she thought it was his picture. She wouldn't know for sure until she actually met him.

And she would never meet him if she didn't move from the entranceway and head into the restaurant. To actually meet him. In person.

Doubt filled her once more and she ruthlessly pushed it away. The time for doubt was gone. Now it was time for action.

She pulled in a deep, bracing breath and smoothed one hand along her skirt. The hostess gave her another judging look but Beth ignored it and sailed right past her. Confidence was everything. She needed to remember that: walk with her head high, a small smile on her lips, her shoulders back.

Walk with an attitude that screamed she was confident and self-assured and filled with purpose. She could do this, she knew she could.

Some of her confidence drained away when she reached the bar area off to the side of the restaurant. Her gaze skimmed the patrons sitting on the leather-covered stools surrounding the varnished bar. Not a single one of them looked familiar. That meant he'd either sent a picture that wasn't his—

Or he wasn't here.

Disappointment filled her as quickly as her confidence fled. Had she really thought she could do this? Had she really thought she could attract the attention of someone who looked like the guy she'd met online?

Isn't that what I told you? Worthless, only good for one thing—

Beth clenched her jaw and told the deep voice to get lost. She certainly didn't need *him* coming into her mind and flaming her biggest fears. She'd been free of him for nine months, she wasn't about to let him come back now, not after all this time.

That didn't stop the disappointment though, or the self-doubt. Had she really expected her online date to show up?

Yes, she had. Even if this *wasn't* a date. The online site she'd recently discovered had been for meeting people, but *not* for dating. It was a hook-up site, more of a chatroom, really. Nothing more than that.

So she shouldn't be disappointed. A lot of things could have happened. Maybe she'd just been played.

Maybe the guy wasn't interested at all.

Maybe he'd found someone better looking—
Stop.

So tonight hadn't worked out. No big deal. It didn't mean anything. She could try again tomorrow, or next week. And in the meantime, she'd just go home and do what she always did—satisfy herself. She didn't have to worry about small talk, didn't have to worry about shaving her legs. Didn't have to worry about any mess—

"Beth?" The voice was deliciously deep and soft and warm. And hesitant. She spun around then had to force herself not to jump up and down and scream with excited glee.

It was *him*. He was actually here! And he looked even more delicious in person.

Tall—tall enough that she had to tilt her head back to really look at him, which meant he was maybe an inch over six feet since she was wearing heels. And his eyes. Oh wow. The picture hadn't even come close to doing his eyes justice: deep, dark blue. So dark they were almost black in the dim light. Blonde hair, darker than the color of sand, framed a face with high cheekbones and a rugged jaw. His hair was thick, a little shaggy, and looked like it might have a tendency to curl. He reminded her of a sun-loving surfer, or maybe even a beach boy.

Except he was no boy. No, he was definitely all man.

Her fingers itched with the desire to run through that hair, to see if it was as thick and soft as it looked. To run along the open V of the blue dress shirt and play with the tiniest patch of darker hair adorning the tanned flesh of his broad chest. To trace the buttons of that shirt down to where they disappeared into the waistband of his dark gray slacks.

But she couldn't do any of that. She could barely get her tongue unstuck from the roof of her mouth.

"Beth?" He repeated her name, the question in his voice even more pronounced, more uncertain. She finally nodded, tried to say *yes* only it came out as a pathetic little stammer. He either didn't notice, or he was too polite to say anything about it. A small smile tilted the corners of his mouth and he stuck out his hand.

"I'm Adam."

Oh, good Lord, no wonder Eve fell into sin.

Beth blinked, worried that maybe she had said that out loud. But no, she must not have because Adam was still standing there, smiling down at her, his hand still outstretched.

She reached for it, felt his fingers close over hers in a firm yet gentle shake. Strong, confident, his skin warm and slightly calloused—not limp and slimy like some handshakes she received. The callouses reassured her for some reason, made him seem more *real*. It was a stupid thing to think, with no basis in anything but fantasy.

That didn't make it any less true.

And it didn't stop the nerves that had been doing somersaults in her stomach all day. The man in front of her, smiling down at her as his thumb stroked the back of her hand, was gorgeous. Not quite an Adonis—no, *better* than an Adonis. And he wanted to meet up with *her*? But why?

Beth almost asked him, almost blurted out the damning word that would expose her lack of confidence with three little letters. She didn't get the chance because Adam released her hand and gently took hold of her elbow.

"Would you like to get a drink? Talk a little?"

Beth nodded then realized he was already leading them toward the bar, his hand a gentle weight in the middle of her back. And he was steering her to a small high top table in the corner, away from the scattered crowd sitting around the bar.

He held the chair out for her then helped her into it, since she had to kind of climb up on it—not the easiest thing to do while wearing a skirt and heels. He waved to one of the servers then leaned across the table, those dark blue eyes totally focused on her.

"What would you like?"

You, naked and on top of me.

Beth swallowed back the words and let her own smile break free. "A white wine?" Maybe the wine would relax her, help her feel not quite so...tense. Or worried. Or nervous.

Adam nodded then turned to give the server their order: a white wine for her, a beer for him.

And then they were alone again and Beth had no idea what to say or how to act. Cool and nonchalant, like she'd done this kind of thing before? If only it were that easy! But she'd never done this kind of thing before and had no idea how to act or what to expect.

Okay, maybe that wasn't entirely true. She knew—mostly—what to *expect*. They were here to hook-up, in the truest sense of the word. They were meeting to have sex, nothing more than that.

So yeah, she knew what to *expect*—later. She just had no idea what to do between now and then.

"Your picture doesn't do you justice."

"Are you kidding me?" As soon as the disbelieving

words left her mouth, she wished she could take them back. She was trying to act confident. Smooth. Worldly. Blurting out disbelief in a dryly humorous voice wasn't part of the plan.

But maybe Adam found it humorous because he chuckled, the sound warm and rich and doing dangerous things to her insides.

"No, I'm pretty serious. Your picture was nice but the in-person version is nicer. Your hair is darker. And your eyes are stunning. I can't quite figure out what color they are."

"Oh. They're ha—"

"No, don't tell me. I want to study them later by candlelight, see if I can figure it out."

And okay, wow. Blood surged through her at his words, heating her, stirring to life an aching need and desire that had been suppressed for too long. Simple words, not even what she would call exceptionally charming. Considering what they were going to do in a little bit, they were even unnecessary. That didn't stop her body's reaction to them.

The server showed up with their drinks, stopping her from having to reply—which was a good thing because Beth had no idea what to say. Adam's words had left her...flustered. Yes, that was as good a word as any.

She took a sip of wine, trying to hide her flush behind the glass. Adam held the bottle of beer between his large hands, spinning it slowly between his palms. But he wasn't looking at the beer, he was looking at her, watching her with those deep blue eyes.

"So tell me a little about yourself, Beth."

Her face heated again, just at the sound of her name wrapped in his velvety voice. She took another small sip of wine then placed the glass on the table in front of her. Was he merely making small talk? Or was he honestly curious? She didn't understand what his motivation was. They were here for the hook-up and nothing more, right? She hadn't really expected the drinks, even if they had agreed to meet at the restaurant attached to the hotel. Beth had figured it was merely a matter of convenience. Or maybe just a matter of appearances because wouldn't it look tacky to just go straight up to the room and get down to business?

But what did she know? She'd never done anything like this before so maybe this was how things were done.

"Well, I work as a hairdresser up in York. I like reading but I don't have as much time for it as I'd like."

"What kind of books do you like?"

"Mystery. Some horror. And romance, of course."

Adam's lips curled into a small smile. "Horror *and* romance? Not together, I hope."

Beth laughed, the sound soft and breathy. "No, not together. How about you? Do you like to read?"

"I'm more into movies. Action and adventure, comedies, things like that. When I read, it's more for work. Manuals and procedurals. Boring stuff."

"What kind of manuals?"

Adam shrugged, the motion almost embarrassed somehow, and looked down at the bottle in his hand. "Building construction. Fire protection. Things like that."

"For work? What do you do?"

He took a quick swig of beer then offered her another embarrassed shrug. "I'm a firefighter."

Beth's gaze dropped to the table. Heat filled her face when she realized she was trying to look below his waist. At least a dozen comments sprung to mind, all of them relating to things he might be able to do with his hose. And oh God, how cliché and pitiful was that? She forced her gaze back to his, saw the way he was watching her with those deep eyes. Another smile teased the corners of his mouth, like he knew exactly what she was thinking.

"Yeah. I'm pretty good at handling my hose. And there's never been a fire I haven't been able to put out."

Oh, my.

Beth reached for her wine glass, nearly knocked it over before her shaking fingers finally wrapped around the slender stem. Need flared to life, filling her with a heat that scorched every nerve ending. She pressed her thighs together, trying to still the wet heat growing between her legs. There were so many things she wanted to say but she couldn't get the words out. Probably a good thing, because none of them were appropriate.

Or maybe they were, if the way Adam was watching her meant anything. Like she was the most desirable creature he'd ever seen. Like he couldn't wait to be alone with her. Like he was more than willing to extinguish the fire raging inside her—but only after it had burned her to a crisp.

The danger of her situation crystallized with each second his gaze held hers. Not the danger of what she was doing by meeting a complete stranger for sex—no, she'd always been aware of that. And even though she shouldn't, even though she knew there was no logical reason for it, she somehow sensed she was safe with Adam.

At least, physically.

The danger lie elsewhere. She knew, with as much

certainty as she'd ever known anything before, that she wouldn't be able to hide from Adam. That if she went upstairs with him, he wouldn't be satisfied until he'd stripped her down to her bare soul.

Just as she knew that he'd give her the same. That she would be with *him*, in so many more ways than just physically.

At least for tonight. For as long as they were together—tonight. A few hours, maybe longer. Maybe even until morning's light. But no more than that.

Never more than that.

Could she do it? Could she allow herself to be laid bare for even that short amount of time?

Her mouth dried and her pulse raced—not from fear, but from excitement. Her skin prickled with awareness, every molecule of her being springing to life with heady anticipation. She wanted to feel his body against hers. No, this was much more than *want*. She *needed* to feel it, as much as she needed to breathe.

It made no sense. She knew that. Just like she knew that the hindsight that came with morning might paint an entirely different picture. But Beth didn't care. Not now, not after the last nine months. Yes, she might regret all of this come morning.

But she didn't care.

She drained her wine and carefully placed the empty glass on the table. Adam's intense gaze remained focused on her as she carefully slid out of the chair and moved to stand next to him. She reached out and placed one trembling hand on his arm.

"Never, hm? Then I think you're definitely the right man for the job."

Chapter Two

She'd never done this before. Ever.

Adam knew that without being told. It was obvious from the way her eyes darted around the hallway as they stepped off the elevator. In the way her fingers trembled ever so slightly against his. In the way her lips tilted in a crooked smile that sent a wave of protectiveness crashing over him.

Beth was nervous but didn't want to let him see it. He thought of saying something to reassure her then decided against it. She was trying so hard to hide it, so hard to act like this was something she was used to. He wanted to let her think he didn't know. If she wanted to confess once they were in the room, then fine. But that was up to her—he didn't want to take that sense of control away from her. Any words he might offer as reassurance might do the exact opposite, so it was better not to say anything.

Actions spoke louder than words, anyway, so it was best to let his actions do the talking. And they would, as soon as they reached his room.

This might not be Adam's first time—not even close. The chatroom he frequented was perfect for his needs: encounters of the purely physical kind, with no strings and no expectations. Mutual satisfaction with no regrets. And most importantly: no commitments.

That didn't mean he didn't take care of his partners. He did. Yes, he was looking for release without commitment—that didn't mean taking advantage. He was a considerate lover, had been told that more than once. And why shouldn't he be? He loved women. Loved their bodies, loved their reactions. The way they felt, the way they smelled. He loved everything about them. So yes, he took his time. These encounters weren't just about him. If all he wanted was a quick release, he could take care of that himself. He wanted more than that: he wanted the physical intimacy, the physical connection.

Just no commitment.

He'd met with several women more than once. Why not, if they were compatible? But never more than three times. That was his rule. More than that and he ran the risk of running into emotional complications. That was the last thing he wanted.

Physical connection, yes. A relationship? Oh hell no, not even close. He saw too much shit at work, both in the field and at the station. Relationships made you vulnerable and weak. And some relationships put you through hell. He didn't need that.

So this was the best of both worlds, no matter what some of the guys on his shift said. Of course, the ones who gave him shit were the ones in those same hellish relationships, so what did they know?

Not a damn thing.

And why the fuck was he thinking about the guys

at work when he was minutes away from a wonderful night with the woman walking beside him? She was beautiful, but not in the way too many men—and women—defined beautiful. Short, maybe only a few inches or more above five feet without the heels she was wearing. She had a body made for loving, with generous curves in all the right places, exactly where a woman should have them. And she didn't try to hide them, didn't cover herself in baggy, shapeless, drab clothes. Did she know how sexy that was? The way she dressed with such confidence? He'd be sure to tell her—to show her—tonight.

Just like he'd show her how gorgeous he thought her hair was. Thick and dark, falling in soft waves past her shoulders. Wide expressive eyes in a color that changed with the light of her mood. Hazel, he was sure, even though he told her he wanted to discover their color later. And he did, he hadn't been lying about that. Watching the way the color seemed to change had intrigued him.

And her mouth. She had a beautiful mouth, almost as expressive as her eyes. Full lips that begged a man to kiss them, taste them. He'd had to fight for control every time he imagined how those lips would feel wrapped around his cock. Yeah, he definitely wanted to feel that, and hoped to hell he'd get the chance tonight.

But he wouldn't push for it, no matter how much he wanted it. Some women enjoyed performing oral sex, others didn't. He had no idea which category Beth fell in.

He'd find out soon enough.

He pulled the key card from his front pocket and waved it in front of the door. The green light flashed with a small *click* and he pushed the door open, stepping out of the way to let Beth move past him. He heard her small gasp, felt the tremor that moved through her when she stopped in front of him.

He had come up to the room earlier, to set things up and make sure everything was ready. The room was lit with the soft flickering light of a dozen different candles. Unscented, because he'd discovered that not all women enjoyed the variety of fragrances. Soft music played from the phone attached to the docking station that doubled as a clock next to the king size bed. An ice-filled stand held an open bottle of white wine. He'd taken a chance with that one and had silently breathed a sigh of relief when Beth had ordered white wine downstairs.

She glanced around the room, her mouth slightly opened in shock, then reached up and tucked a strand of hair behind her ear. Adam sensed her uncertainty and offered her a small smile before moving to the stand and pulling out the bottle. He poured two glasses and walked back to her, his arm outstretched as he offered her one of the glasses.

"You, uh, don't take any chances, do you?"

"Chances?" Adam looked around the room then turned back to her and shrugged. "I never considered being romantic taking a chance."

"I guess I never considered that a hook-up could be romantic."

"Why should they be mutually exclusive?"

She opened her mouth, then closed it with a frown. Adam waited but she didn't speak, obviously changing her mind about saying whatever she had been about to say. He stayed where he was, simply watching her as she took several nervous sips of the wine.

Minutes drifted by, filled with the strains of soft music. He sensed her tension drifting away, watched as her body slowly relaxed. He stepped closer, eased the glass from her hand and placed it on the nightstand closest to him. He didn't wait, didn't ask permission, just reached for her hands and drew her against him. Her head tilted back and her eyes drifted closed. Was she expecting a kiss?

Yes. But not yet.

He wrapped one arm low around her back and laced his fingers through one of her hands, guiding it to his chest. Then he led her into a slow dance, their bodies swaying to the music. Her lids fluttered open, surprise flashing in her eyes when she looked at him. Adam simply smiled and pulled her closer as the music wrapped around them.

Her body relaxed even more, the trembling in her fingers slowly disappearing as they moved in a small circle near the bed. He released her hand, pressed it against his chest in a silent demand that she not move it, then gently slid his fingers through her hair. Thick, smooth. Soft. He rubbed the silky strands between his thumb and finger, marveling at the texture. A small sigh escaped her parted lips. She closed her eyes and tilted her head to the side, exposing the smooth column of her throat. Her pulse beat against the pale skin, a steady *thump thump thump* that he could see even in the dim light.

He lowered his head and pressed his lips against the fragile pulse beat. Beth stiffened in his arms, but only for a second before tilting her head further to the side. Adam tightened his arm around her, fitting her body more closely to his, and ran his lips along her neck. A shiver ran across her skin, a sigh escaping her as he kissed his way to her jaw and ear, lower to the muscled cord connecting neck and shoulder. Another shiver, this one longer as she pressed herself even closer.

Adam pulled away and looked down at her through heavy-lidded eyes. Her face was flushed, those full lips still parted, her eyes partially closed. He ran his fingers through her hair again, the thick waves curling around his hand.

"Are you okay?" His voice was thick and husky, a little hoarse. Her lids fluttered open, her gaze slowly meeting his. A smile curled the corners of her mouth and she slowly nodded.

Adam answered her smile with one of his own, his fingers still stroking her hair. "If you need me to stop, just say so."

"I'm—" She stopped, cleared her throat. "I'm okay."

"Good. If there's anything you don't like, let me know. If there's anything you want, let me know."

She nodded, her gaze darting to the open collar of his shirt before shooting back to his. The flush on her face deepened, her teeth nibbling on her full lower lip. He saw shyness he hadn't expected to see, mixed with a hungry need. A wave of desire crashed over him but he held himself still, not wanting to scare her.

Wanting her to tell him what she wanted.

Her trembling fingers stroked the material of his dress shirt, tiny little circles on his chest just above the pounding of his heart. She looked away, took a deep breath that pressed the fullness of her breasts against him, then looked back.

Still shy, still hesitant—but a little bolder, too.

"I'd like to..." Her voice trailed off and she looked

away again. Adam didn't move, his breath held as he waited to see what she would say. If she would say anything. She took another deep breath, her gaze finally moving back to his. Her tongue darted out, swiped along her lower lip, leaving it moist and plump.

"I—I'd like you to lose the shirt."

Adam released his hold on her and stepped back, then spread his arms out to the side. His gaze held hers, his silent message clear. She watched him for several long seconds, her eyes changing from light brown to a darker green. Or maybe it was just a trick of the flickering candles that made it seem her eyes were changing colors. Adam didn't care—they were beautiful. Mesmerizing.

Her hands reached for him, her fingers brushing against his chest as she undid the first button of his shirt. Then the second, and the third. Slow, so slow. Was she deliberately teasing him? Or was that merely hesitation? He didn't care, not when the back of her hand brushed against the bare skin of his chest. Once, twice. Again, lower, as she pulled the hem of the shirt from his trousers and undid the last two buttons. She stepped closer, spreading his shirt wider, then lightly ran her hands over his bare flesh. Her fingers teased the light dusting of hair on his chest, traced the pale line that trailed down his abdomen. Back up, her touch less hesitant, growing bolder.

Adam sucked in a sharp breath and closed his eyes, his jaw clenched and his head tilted back as she pressed her mouth against his heated flesh. Soft, tantalizing, her kisses trailing liquid fire along his skin.

He shrugged out of the shirt, saw her gaze dart to his arms. She ran her hands up his chest, along the width of his shoulders and down his arms, her mouth once again raining gentle kisses on his skin.

His cock hardened even more, throbbed almost painfully as it pushed against the zipper of his trousers. Excitement, desire. All of that and more, merely from her shy kisses and touches.

He stepped closer, captured her face between his hands, and closed his mouth over hers. Gently at first, learning the curves of her full lips, tasting the sweetness of her mouth. He ran his tongue along the seam of her lips, sighed as her mouth opened under his. Sweet, like the wine she'd had earlier. Heady and intoxicating. He deepened the kiss, explored the dark recess of her mouth, drinking in her sweetness.

Kissing, never stopping, losing himself in her taste and touch.

He trailed his finger along her face, across her jaw and throat. Lower, tracing the outline of her collarbone, her shoulder. Down along her side, to the swell of one full breast, lower to the flare of her rounded hip. Back up, catching the hem of her sweater in his fist and dragging it up. His knuckles grazed soft flesh, warm and smooth; brushed against the silky lace encasing her breasts.

He broke the kiss, his gaze holding hers as he pulled the sweater over her head and tossed it to the side. Her hands came up, trying to cover herself as he drank in the sight of creamy flesh hidden by dark green lace. He grabbed her hands, pulled them away and caught her gaze once more.

"Let me look."

Her teeth pulled at her lower lip, her expression shy and uncertain once more. She finally nodded, the barest movement of her head. In answer to him, or to herself? It didn't matter, not when the tension eased from her body.

Adam offered her a small smile then let his gaze drift across her body, down to the creamy fullness of her breasts. The points of her nipples pressed against the lace, hardening even more under his gaze. He released her hands, traced the delicate collarbone with one finger, ran it down to the swell of her breast. The lace of her bra teased the pad of his finger, a contradiction from the smoothness of plump flesh above the scalloped edge. Back and forth, smooth skin and textured lace, a difference that somehow enthralled him.

He brushed his thumb against the hardened peak of her nipple, his cock tightening in response to her small gasp. Her body stiffened, relaxed once more as he continued stroking the tight bud. His hand cupped the fullness of her breast, its weight filling his palm. He slid his finger along the edge of her bra once more, dipped it between the deep valley of her cleavage before moving to the other breast.

Her chest rose and fell with each breath, shorter and faster as he continued to learn the weight and feel of each breast. He reached for her hands, led her to the bed and lowered himself to the edge and positioned her so she was standing between his legs. His gaze met hers, held it for the space of several rapid heartbeats. Then he leaned forward and pressed his mouth against her, his tongue teasing the hardened peak through the lace.

She gasped again, the sound short and sharp. Her hands reached out, tangled in his hair, holding him in place. He smiled, pulled the nipple deeper into his mouth, sucking harder. She gasped again, her hips gently thrusting forward with each pull.

"You like that?"

"Yes." The answer was nothing more than a breathy sigh, filled with a need and hunger that caused his cock to ache. He grabbed the edges of lace and pulled them down over her breasts, exposing the creamy fullness to his sight, his touch.

He wrapped his hands around each breast, closed his mouth over one nipple, and feasted on her taste. Sucking, nibbling, each little gasp sending flames of desire through his tight body.

He dragged his hand along her side, across the flare of full, shapely hips, down further to the hem of her skirt. He dipped his hand inside, ran his palm up along the flesh of her inner thigh. Higher, higher still. He expected to feel the rough texture of lace covering her. Instead, he found bare flesh. Smooth, soft, supple. Hot and wet.

Adam groaned at the heat pressed against his hand. He sucked harder on her nipple, teasing the tight bud with tongue and teeth as he ran his finger along her clit. She moaned, pressed her hips into his touch, her hands fisting in his hair.

He gave her nipple one long pull then leaned back, watching her as he stroked the sensitive flesh between her legs. Her head was tilted back, her eyes closed, her mouth parted. Her chest rose and fell with each breath, her hips rocking against his touch.

"Take your skirt off for me. Let me see you."

Her lids fluttered open, her eyes glazed as she looked down at him. Hesitation flashed in their depths, the shyness returning. But only for a second. She stepped away, reached behind her to undo the zipper of the skirt. Her thumbs dipped into the waistband, her gaze darting back to his as she hesitated again.

Then she pushed the skirt over her hips, the material sliding past her thighs to pool in a puddle at her feet. She pulled her lower lip between her teeth, her gaze steady on his, then kicked the skirt away.

Adam's gaze wandered over her body, drinking in every inch of flushed skin. The heavy fullness of her breasts, still encased in green lace. The gentle swell of her abdomen. The flare of full hips and creamy thighs and shapely calves. A woman's body, ripe and enchanting, designed for carnal feasting.

His gaze traveled back up, met hers again. He offered her a smile of silent appreciation then reached out and traced the flare of her hip with his palm. Lower, moving between her legs, cupping her bare pussy.

"Delectable." His voice was thick, husky, filled with need. He swallowed back a groan as her hips moved against his hand, her legs parting for him.

Adam dropped to his knees, wrapped one arm around her hips, and pressed his mouth against her wet heat. So fucking wet. So fucking hot.

So fucking sweet.

He slid one finger inside her, felt her muscles tighten around him as he ran his tongue along her clit. She sighed, the sound sharp and needy as her fingers dug into his shoulders. Her hips thrust again, faster, as he plunged his finger into her. Deeper. In, out. His tongue stroked her, faster, matching the rhythm of her thrusts.

He slid another finger into her wet heat, felt her body shudder and heard her gasp in surprise. Faster. Harder, deeper, fingers and tongue stroking. Drinking from her, tasting her sweetness as her body came to life. Her nails dug deeper into the flesh of his shoulders, her sighs and moans coming faster. Adam didn't stop, continued driving her to the edge and holding her there. Over and over, adjusting each touch, each lick, pulling back just before she could plummet into fulfillment.

She called his name, her raspy voice filled with urgent need. Her hips thrust against his touch. Seeking. Demanding. He drove his fingers deeper, pulled her clit between his teeth and sucked.

A scream ripped from her chest, her body shuddering as her muscles clamped around him. Pulling, holding...shattering. She screamed again, the sound thick and raspy as she clung to him. He tightened his arm around her hips, supporting her, holding her upright when her knees started buckling. But he didn't stop, not until her climax started easing. Not until she pushed against him, her weak voice begging him for mercy.

Adam pushed to his feet, sweeping her into his arms and turning toward the bed in one fluid motion. He gently placed her on the mattress then quickly removed the rest of his clothes, standing over, watching her body as it slowly stilled, replete and satisfied.

She stretched, her back arching, the nipples of her breasts proud and erect. Her lids fluttered open, her gaze drifting to his. Her eyes widened, her skin flushing as she noticed him watching her. She scooted back, one arm moving to cover herself as she pushed up on her elbow. Her gaze drifted down, settling on the swollen length of his cock. Her tongue darted out, hunger filling her eyes.

Adam swallowed a groan, his own carnal hunger searing his veins as she watched him. He closed his fist over the length of his cock, stroking. Slow and hard, from the base to the tip and back again. Beth's eyes widened even more, darkening with passion and need. She reached out, her trembling hand closing over his, her thumb grazing the tip of his cock as he continued stroking.

He groaned, closed his eyes and let his head fall back as her hand closed over him, taking his place. Her touch was like velvet, soft and smooth, wrapping him in gentle heat.

Adam held himself still, struggling to control his breathing. Struggling to control his reaction. What was it about her touch that threatened to shatter his control? Not innocent, but hesitant. Still shy, still uncertain. And so powerful, it threatened to send him over the edge. God help him if she took his throbbing cock into her mouth because he wasn't sure he would be able to control his response if she did.

He groaned, fisted his hand over hers and gently eased it away. He heard her whimper of disappointment and quickly leaned forward, his mouth closing over hers to stifle any question she might have.

He kneeled on the bed, their mouths still melded together, and followed her down to the mattress. Downy softness surrounded them as heated flesh met heated flesh. Soft, firm, warm and welcoming. He rolled to the side, shifted Beth in his arms then rolled to his back so she straddled him. His cock pressed against her wet heat and the temptation to drive into her, to grab her hips and thrust his cock deep inside her, was strong. So strong it almost frightened him.

He groaned again, shifting her body to move the temptation away. He leaned to the side, his hand closing over one of the condoms on the nightstand.

Within seconds, his cock was sheathed and ready.

He shifted Beth over him, rocked his hips so his cock slid against her clit. Still wet from her climax, still swollen and ready. He ran his hands along her sides, cupped her breasts and squeezed them together then teased each nipple between his thumb and forefinger. Beth gasped, the sound ending in a sharp sigh as she pressed herself against him.

Adam grabbed her hips, shifting her one last time then holding her still as he drove his cock into her. And oh fuck, she was so fucking wet. So fucking tight. Her body fit around his, pulling him in. Her muscles squeezed around him, as if afraid he would leave.

Not a fucking chance of that happening. Not anytime soon.

He bent his legs and braced his heels against the mattress, his grip tightening around her hips as he drove into her. Harder, faster. Deep, so fucking deep. She leaned back, her hands braced against his thighs, her hips pumping against his. He held himself still, letting her set the pace, rejoicing in each thrust, in each squeeze along his cock.

And fuck, she felt so good. A perfect fit for him, better than any of the other women he'd had in the past. Beyond perfect, almost heaven. She kept riding him, faster and faster, her full breasts bouncing with the rhythm. Her head tilted back, the ends of her hair brushing along his thighs. Teasing, sending another kind of sensation shooting through him.

She continued to move, her pussy clenching his cock with each thrust of her hips. Breaths turned to rasps, morphed into gasps and sharp moans. His hands tightened even more, his fingers digging into the flesh of her full thighs. Guiding her now, over and over, faster, his gaze focused on the sight of his cock disappearing into her wet pussy with each thrust.

And fuck, he was so close. So fucking close to exploding. But not yet, not until she came. Not until he felt her climaxing, felt her pussy clench around him over and over with her own orgasm.

He pushed into her, the strength of his drive nearly lifting her from the bed. Her gasp was short, surprised. Breathy and sharp. He did it again, over and over, driving into her, hard and fast. Harder. Harder still until her breath escaped as a scream. Her hips rocked, the rhythm choppy and almost desperate as she came. Nails scored the flesh of his thighs, sending a wave of excitement shooting through him, straight to his cock. He drove into her again, harder, heard her scream his name as his own climax exploded with a blinding force that left him struggling for breath.

And holy fuck, he couldn't breathe. Couldn't remember the last time he'd had such an intense orgasm. Hell, he could barely remember his own fucking name.

All he knew was that tonight wouldn't be enough. Even two more nights might not be enough.

But he'd have to make them enough because no matter how fucking intense being with Beth was, he would never break his own rule.

Never.

Chapter Three

Darkness. Heat. Scorching, prickling the skin of his exposed neck. Adam made a low sound in the back of his throat, a growl that was lost in the roar of the fire creeping closer to them.

He reached behind him, his hands closing over the charged line and moving it forward, playing it out so Mikey could advance. The squawk of a radio screeched in his ear, the words mumbled and incoherent. Over that was Mikey's voice, a little higher pitched and filled with determination.

"Fuck that shit!" Mikey crawled forward, moving a little faster, then leaned on her elbows and opened the nozzle. The spray turned to steam before hitting the flames. Heat intensified, pushing them closer to the floor.

Any fucking closer and they'd be on the floor below.

The radio squawked to life again, the sound distorted and unintelligible. Adam strained his ears but the only words he could make out were Mikey's shouts.

Broken, muffled through the mask, the tone belligerent and pissed.

The room grew hotter, flames lapping the ceiling overhead in spite of the water shooting from the nozzle. And fuck, this was getting hot. Too hot. If they didn't stop it in the next minute, he and Mikey both would be crispier than the burgers Jay had burnt at dinner.

Adam moved forward, his legs and stomach burning from the heat of the water pooling beneath him. His hand closed over Mikey's foot, trailed up the leg covered in gear, stopped dangerously close to her ass.

"Damn good thing Nick likes you or he'd have your head for grabbing my ass like that."

Despite the seriousness of their situation, Adam had to swallow back a bark of laughter. So what if he was damn near sprawled on top of Mikey? She was just one of the guys. He was sure Nick would understand either way.

"Mikey, we need to pull back."
"Bullshit."
"Stop being so fucking stubborn."
"We can get this—"
"Dammit Mikey—"

The radio came to life, blaring in their ears. Somewhere in the distance, he heard the sound of an air horn: three short blasts, faint and faraway. He tilted his head, listening. The horns blared again, somehow more urgent this time.

"Mikey—"

"Yeah. Go. Go, go." She backed up, turned around, and pushed him ahead of her. The radio blared to life once more and she shouted into it, each word clear, her voice calm but still frustrated.

"Ten-four, we're on our way." Something smacked his ass, the touch barely discernible through the heavy gear. "You wanted to go? Now's your chance. Get moving."

Adam swallowed back a bark of laughter and picked up the pace, following the hose line as he moved it through the darkness in front of him. Back up the hallway, across a landing, down the first flight of steps. A little faster as the heat closed in on them, still searing and scorching. Another flight of steps, closer to the exit.

The smoke was thicker, the heat just as intense. The door should be close by, they should be able to see a little better by now. But it was getting even darker, the heat even more intense. The back of his neck prickled, his senses tingling. Something wasn't right, something—

"Mikey—"

"Yeah, I know. Go. Move. Now." Her voice was still calm, controlled. But he didn't miss the urgency under the words. He moved faster, Mikey right behind him, pushing. The shadow of the doorway loomed in front of them, growing larger. Another shadow appeared, separating into two smaller ones. Hands grabbed him, pulling and pushing and shoving.

And then they were outside, rolling away from the flames that had followed them. A heavy weight landed on top of him, pushing the air from his lungs as the bottle dug into his back. He grunted and reached up, pushing off his helmet and removing his facemask.

Mikey was sprawled across him, half-straddling him, her breathing heavy as she pushed the hood off and removed her own facemask. She looked down at him, a crooked smile spreading across her soot-covered face as she squirmed against him.

"Damn Adam. I'm impressed. I didn't realize what you were hiding down here."

"You're a fucking perv, Mikey. Anyone ever tell you that?"

"Yeah—Nick. Every damn night." She wiggled her eyebrows then rolled off him and pushed to her knees, slightly bent over at the waist. A grimace crossed her face then she sucked in a deep breath and shook her head, her ponytail swinging behind her.

"You okay?"

"Hm?" She turned, a flicker of surprise crossing her face, as if she just realized he was sitting there beside her. "Yeah. Fine." She pushed to her feet then extended her hand, helping Adam to his feet.

He didn't believe her and was getting ready to push for a better answer when Jay approached them. His face was dirty and sweaty, from the fire and from the warmth of the early September air. His pale gray eyes were tired, filled with a combination of frustration and worry.

"What the fuck, Mikey? We were getting ready to come in after you. Why the hell—"

"We were fine. We had it." Mikey waved off his concern and moved past him, dragging the hose line with her. Jay's face turned red, his jaw clenching in anger. Or maybe impatience. Or maybe both. He tossed a look at Adam but Adam just shook his head and grabbed the hose, helping Mikey move it away from the building. No way in hell was he getting in the middle of whatever spat was brewing between them. Not those two.

He'd been assigned to Station 14 for almost two

years and still didn't exactly understand the dynamics between Jay Moore and Michaela Donaldson. When he'd first been transferred there, he had sworn the two were an actual couple. As in, *together*. They were extremely close, always together, able to share a wealth of communication with a single glance. But they were nothing more than good friends—*real* friends, not the kind with benefits.

Mikey was engaged to her high school sweetheart, the couple reunited after a decade of separation. Adam still wasn't sure of the all the details, only knew there had been some kind of accident or traumatic experience or something that had broken the two apart more than ten years ago. They'd met again through a bizarre series of coincidences and were now engaged to be married—even though they still hadn't set a date.

And Jay had bought a house not too long ago and was currently living with his girlfriend—who just happened to be the sister of one of their paramedics, Dave Warren. And yeah, hadn't *that* been fun, when the entire thing blew up and Jay and Dave had nearly killed each other, right there in the engine room once Dave found out about it. *Tense* didn't even begin to describe the whole damn scenario.

But things had worked out somehow. At least, Dave and Jay seemed to be getting along. For the most part. Which was probably a good thing because even though there was no talk of a wedding yet, Adam was sure it was just a matter of time before Jay popped the question and asked Angie to marry him.

And sorry, but no, thank you. That so wasn't for him. After seeing the ups-and-downs and all the drama and tension of his co-workers' relationships, Adam was even more convinced that whole relationship thing wasn't for him. He was quite happy with the way things were going for him: casual hook-ups, no strings, no commitments. And absolutely no drama.

He dropped the line as they reached the engine then moved around the back, releasing the straps of his bottle as he went. He and Mikey lowered them to the ground at the same time and damn if he didn't see Mikey grimace again. Jay saw it, too, because he frowned and moved closer to her.

"You okay?"

"Christ, you're as bad as Adam. What are you two, mother hens? I'm fine."

"You don't look fine. And you were grabbing your stomach—"

"I'm *fine*." Mikey leaned closer to Jay, impatience flaring in her eyes. "It's cramps. I'm PMSing. You want more details? Because I can give them to you—"

"No!" Jay and Adam said it at the same time then shared a quick glance and started laughing. Mikey rolled her eyes and mumbled something—probably an insult or some shit like that, knowing her.

No way was Adam going to ask her to repeat herself. Not that it mattered because Pete Miller, their Lieutenant, came trotting toward them, his coat hanging open, his blue helmet sitting at an angle on his head.

"You two—" He wagged a finger between Adam and Mikey. "Get over to rehab. Get checked out—"

"We don't—"

"I don't want to hear it, Mike. You know the drill. Just do it then get back here. They want us to surround-and-drown. Which means we're going to be here a bit longer."

Shit. Adam turned to study the building, frowning

at the flames licking up the walls from the busted windows. It was a three-story industrial office building, vacant only because it was late on the Saturday evening of Labor Day weekend. Could they have knocked the flames back while they were inside?

Maybe. If the building's sprinkler system had been operating properly. If the call had come in earlier. If there hadn't been an issue with getting water. If, if, if. So many ifs.

Yeah, maybe they could have. Or maybe he and Mikey were lucky not to be stuck inside.

They couldn't second-guess themselves and play what-ifs. There would be enough of the Monday-morning quarterbacking going on once the white hats got together to analyze and evaluate and play out different scenarios.

Adam wasn't worried about that. And he knew without looking that neither was the rest of his crew. They'd come in and tried to do their job as best as they could—for as long as they were allowed. And no matter what else might happen, he was certain of two things. First, the white hats would find some kind of fault with the initial crews on the scene. And second— they were going to be here for quite a while. Probably all night.

Which meant he was going to miss his chat with Beth. Disappointment hit him in the gut, surprising him. What the fuck? Really? Since when did missing a call with any of his hook-ups worry him?

Maybe it was because it had been three weeks since he'd been with anyone else, since that night with Beth. That in itself should worry him. Maybe he just needed one more time with Beth to get her out of his system.

And maybe it was a damn good thing he *was* missing that call.

"Yo, Adam. Wake up." He turned just as Mikey was punching his shoulder. "What the hell were you daydreaming about?"

"Nothing."

She raised one brow, silently mocking him, letting him know she didn't believe him. It didn't matter because there was no way in hell he'd tell her. The guys gave him enough grief about his dating habits. The last thing any of them needed to know was that he was starting to obsess about his latest hook-up, especially since they'd only been together that one night. He'd never live it down.

So yeah, it was probably a good thing he was missing his chat with Beth. It would probably be even better if he scheduled another hook-up with someone different. Yeah, that would probably be for the best.

But damn if the idea didn't leave him feeling a little hollow inside.

Chapter Four

"Why do you keep looking at your phone?"

Beth stopped reaching for the pocket of her apron and leaned across the table for her water bottle instead. "I'm not."

"Liar." Her best friend and co-worker, Courtney Williams, smiled when she said it. There was no accusation in her quiet voice, just a hint of teasing. Beth still felt guilty though. Not because she had been caught trying to check her phone, but because she'd been checking it *too* often—doing exactly what she swore she wouldn't do.

Exactly what she promised herself she wouldn't do. She didn't want a relationship, especially not after her last disastrous one. But she'd had so much fun with Adam, *feeling* things she hadn't felt in...well, ever. Like she mattered, like he was putting her first.

Which was stupid. It was just sex. *Purely* sex. That was the whole purpose of the hook-up—to have anonymous sex without all the messy drama and emotion. Beth needed to keep reminding herself of that.

It should be easy enough. She hadn't seen Adam since their one night together. They had chatted a few times, very casually. He'd even mentioned the possibility of meeting again. Not for a date—Beth had a feeling that was as much against his rules as it was hers. *If* they saw each other again, it would be for nothing more than another hook-up. Sex. Pure and simple.

They were supposed to chat again this evening, and maybe even set something up for another hook-up. At least, that was the impression Beth got from their last chat. *That's* why she kept checking her phone. But so far, nothing.

And she couldn't tell Courtney any of that. Not because they were at work—they were both on break in the back room of the salon where they worked, waiting for their next appointments. They were like family, everyone that worked there, telling stories and sharing secrets all the time. That didn't matter—this was one secret Beth couldn't share, no matter where they were.

Courtney wouldn't understand, not if Beth told her she had met a complete stranger for the sole purpose of having sex. Courtney was a single mom of an adorable two-year-old boy, and she took her parenting responsibilities seriously. She didn't date, at all. She rarely went out, even for girls' night. Her whole life revolved around Noah. Beth admired her for it and knew it couldn't be easy, raising a young child at the age of twenty-one—especially a deaf child. Beth had no idea who Noah's father was or what had happened that he wasn't in the picture. Courtney stubbornly refused to talk about him, no matter how many times

Beth asked—which she rarely did anymore. She couldn't bear to see the sadness that filled her friend's eyes whenever the subject came up. Did Courtney still love him? Probably—whoever the jerk was.

Just one more reason to stay away from relationships. They just weren't worth the potential heartache and drama. If Beth didn't like sex so much, she'd stay home, too, just like Courtney.

Which was why she'd finally decided to do the whole hook-up thing: all the benefits of sex without the messy relationship business.

Except here she was, waiting for a text from Adam in the hopes of getting together again.

"So are you going to tell me or not?" Courtney was still watching her, seeing too much with those sad brown eyes.

"There's nothing to tell."

"Hmm. Why don't I believe that?"

"No idea because it's the truth."

Courtney snorted, the delicate sound filled with disbelief. Then her eyes widened and she leaned forward, wrapping her hand around Beth's wrist. "Please tell me you're not back with Ed."

"Oh my God. No! Not even. I can't believe you'd even think that. I'm not that stupid."

Courtney blew out a sigh of relief and sat back in her chair. "Good. I was worried that you might have changed your mind. Again."

Beth frowned at her use of the word *again*. So maybe she had been stupid, getting back together with him a second time. But that had been nine months ago. She'd finally learned her lesson. "No. Never again. Two strikes and he's so out."

"It should have been one strike. Not even that. I

never liked him." Courtney leaned forward, her gaze intense. "Or the way he treated you. He was so ignorant. And so...so—just ignorant. I hated him."

"But he was so good in bed." Beth had meant for the comment to be lighthearted and breezy, maybe even a little exaggerated. It went right over Courtney's head, though. Either that or her friend chose to ignore it.

"I don't care how good the sex was. That doesn't excuse the way he treated you."

"So says the woman who hasn't had sex in almost three years."

"There are more important things in life besides..." Courtney's voice trailed off and she looked away, a deep blush spreading across her face—probably because Beth was staring at her with her mouth hanging open in shock.

"Please tell me you've at least—"

"I'm not talking about it."

Beth kept watching Courtney, wondering if she should push for an answer or not. Her friend wasn't a prude—not by a long shot. But she also wasn't as open about her private life as Beth was, at least not about the sex part. That didn't mean she hadn't had sex since Noah was born.

Or did it?

As much as Beth really wanted to know, she wouldn't push for a real answer. Not yet, anyway. Knowing her luck, pushing would only backfire on her and they'd end up talking about *Beth's* sex life. And she wasn't about to tell Courtney about the sexy firefighter she'd met for the sole purpose of having sex. Courtney would totally freak then probably give her a lecture.

No, Beth would wait and let Courtney save the

lecture for another time, especially since it was looking more and more like her one night with Adam was just that: one night. And there was nothing wrong with that, not when that was the whole point of hooking up to begin with. Beth just needed to remember that.

Sex. It was nothing more than sex.

If she wanted more, all she had to do was go back into the chatroom and find someone else she could hook-up with. Not a big deal.

And she would. Soon.

Eventually.

"We should go out after work. Go see a movie or something." A movie would be the perfect thing to get her mind off sex. Off Adam. Off sex *with* Adam. But Courtney was shaking her head already.

"I need to get home. Mom is working until eleven and I don't want to leave Noah with the sitter longer than I have to."

"Oh. Sure, no problem. Maybe another night." Beth wasn't as successful at keeping the disappointment from her voice as she thought she was because Courtney gave her a sympathetic look. Then her eyes cleared and a small smile played on her lips.

"We could always have a movie night at my place. Pop some popcorn and eat ice cream. Not the same as going out but—"

"But better than going out. No crowds, right? Sounds like a plan."

"Perfect. What did you want to watch?"

"No idea. We'll find something, though." Beth pushed away from the table and grabbed her water then hesitated. "As long as it's not a romance. I'm so not in the mood for that."

Courtney laughed, the sound somehow strained.

"Trust me, neither am I."

Beth was ready to ask why but Shelly poked her head in the back to let her know her next appointment was here. She nodded and took one last swallow of water before tossing the empty bottle into the recycling bin. She'd have plenty of time tonight to find out why Courtney looked so glum.

And if she was too busy worrying about her friend, she wouldn't have time to mope around feeling sorry for herself because she hadn't heard from Adam.

And maybe, if she was lucky, she'd even be able to convince herself that she didn't want to see him again.

Chapter Five

Water pounded against his back, the lukewarm temperature barely registering in Adam's mind. He was only remotely aware of it, mostly on a subconscious level. Just enough to know, somewhere in the back of his mind, that the spray would turn icy cold in a matter of minutes.

He closed his eyes and tilted his head into the spray. Water poured over his face, ran down his bare chest and abdomen, splashed against the hard length of his cock. He tightened his grip and kept stroking, hard and fast as he massaged his balls with his free hand.

Close. So fucking close.

Beth, kneeling in front of him, her tongue swirling around the tip of his cock. Her nails scoring the flesh of his inner thighs. Her long hair, wet and wild, tangled around her face as she waited, silently begging.

Fuck. So fucking close. He could *feel* her hot breath against his cock as she kneeled there in front of him, her mouth open, waiting to taste him.

He stroked harder, his hand sliding up and down the hard length of his cock. Almost there...so fucking close.

He clenched his jaw, Beth's image seared into his brain as he fisted his hand in the wet tangle of her hair. Positioning her, holding her in place, her mouth open and ready. Her head tilted back, her glazed eyes watching him. Her tongue, moist and pink and so fucking hot, sweeping across her bottom lip before stroking the underside of his cock.

Pleading. Begging. Demanding.

Come for me, Adam. Come for me.

His balls drew tight and his breath froze in his lungs. One firm stroke, hard and fast. One more before his climax seized him, the strength of his release nearly paralyzing him.

He forced his eyes open and looked down. Watched, almost detached, as semen spurted from his cock and hit the porcelain tile of the shower wall.

"Fuck!" The word was ripped from his throat, harsh and reedy. He kept stroking, watching each spurt of cum shoot from his cock. Hot, thick. Over and over until his knees were in danger collapsing and sending him crashing to the shower floor.

But there was no Beth, not here. Only in his mind, part memory and part fantasy.

He pulled in a shuddering breath and released his cock, spun around to face the shower spray. The water was colder now, only minutes away from turning icy. He didn't care, not if it helped dispel the images of Beth that kept popping into his fucking brain.

It wasn't the memories that bothered him—it was the fantasies. Like just now, imagining her on her knees in front of him, her head tilted back as he fisted his hand in her hair and shot his cum into her mouth.

How many times had he gotten himself off to images of Beth in the last few weeks? Too many. More than he wanted to admit to. But nothing like just now. That last orgasm had been...powerful. And his need was almost desperate.

What the fuck was wrong with him?

He grabbed the bar of soap and quickly washed, his teeth chattering from the cold by the time he was finished. But damn if his cock wasn't nearly hard again as he dried himself off.

Need.

Fuck. Adam didn't do *need*, especially not after one night.

Which meant that what he was about to do ranked right up there at the top of his list of *stupid ideas*. If he was smart, he'd go into the den, log into the chatroom, and find another hook-up. Someone close by and available within the hour. They could fuck all night, he'd get it out of his system, and that would be it.

Except he had tried that this morning before his relief had even made it through the door. He'd still been ramped up from the fire last night, his cock half hard and ready to go. He hadn't had a chance to chat with Beth because they'd been on the fire ground for so long the night before. He hadn't been able to set something else up with her, had figured maybe that was the reason he was so ready to go.

So he connected with someone else while he'd been in the kitchen sipping his coffee and waiting for his relief. Everything had been set up—he was going to meet the new girl at a park not too far from the station. Nothing more than a quick fuck, either in the back of his truck, her car. Hell, even in the woods off one of the secluded paths. He didn't care.

He never made it, though. He connected with the girl again—fuck, he couldn't even remember her name—and canceled. Five minutes later, she was back in the chatroom, making another connection. Good for her. He wished to hell he could have done the same thing.

But he couldn't bring himself to change his mind. Couldn't bring himself to make another connection himself, no matter how hard his cock was. And he was afraid to look too closely for the reason why.

Hell, he didn't have to look, not when he couldn't get Beth's image from his mind. And what the fuck was up with that? There was nothing special about her. Short and petite, round with healthy curves in all the right places. Sexy as hell with that air of innocence and uncertainty. Definitely not as experienced as he was used to, but not completely inexperienced, either.

So why the fuck couldn't he stop thinking about her?

Adam ran the towel over his hair, sopping up most of the water before tossing it over his shoulder. He palmed the light switch as he left the bathroom and walked down the hall to the spare room he used as a den, trying to ignore the fact that his cock was already growing hard.

He nudged the mouse and brought the computer to life, then took a seat in the chair and went online. He reached down with his free hand, absently stroking his cock as he entered his password for the chatroom. It should be easy enough to find someone to meet with tonight. If he was lucky, maybe he'd even find someone close enough that they could get down to business in the next thirty minutes.

If he was lucky. He sure as hell hoped so because much more of this and his poor cock would be chafed from jerking off so much. And he had nobody to blame but himself. This was his fault for waiting so long. Not that three weeks was that long—hell, he'd definitely gone without longer. The problem wasn't so much the amount of time as it was that he'd allowed himself to think only of Beth during that time. That *had* to be it. That was the only explanation that made any sense.

He still didn't know *why* and that's what worried him the most. Part of him was afraid to look too closely into it.

But no more. He'd find someone else and take care of things and that would be that. Hell, maybe he would get extra lucky and find two girls to join him. He'd done that once before. The experience had been totally fucking hot, having four hands and two mouths on him—up until the girls had decided they were more into each other than him. Even then it had been exciting, watching them go down on each other, eating each other's pussy, watching them fuck each other with the dildo one of them had brought as he jerked off between them.

But damn, he didn't want to jerk off again. He wanted hot pussy wrapped around his cock as he came, not his hand. He could do that himself.

He glanced down, frowning at the sight of his hand stroking his cock. Hell, he *was* doing that himself. With a growl of impatience, he moved his hand. No more jerking off tonight. If a hand was going to stroke his cock, he wanted it to belong to someone else—someone small and feminine.

A frown creased Adam's face as he scanned the

screen names of everyone in the chatroom. Not for the first time, he wondered if something was wrong with him. Chatrooms, hook-ups. Nameless, faceless sex. Casual encounters. Threesomes and porn. Nobody else he knew was into anything like this, not really. Yeah, they knew he got around. Knew he refused to settle down. He'd mentioned casual hook-ups once a few months ago and had received nothing but odd, questioning looks. He hadn't bothered to mention the rest of it, hadn't bothered to share any details. The expression on everyone's faces had let him know they wouldn't understand, no matter how much Adam might try to explain.

Not that he knew how to. He hadn't always been into casual sex, not since he was a horny teenager. At least, not to this extent. This whole thing—lifestyle, habit, preference, whatever the fuck you wanted to call it—hadn't even been on his radar until about eight months ago.

When he walked in on his girlfriend on her hands and knees in *his* fucking bed being fucked by some other guy. She'd looked horrified at being caught—then turned on as he stood there, watching. Not because he wanted to—because he'd been so fucking shocked he couldn't move at first. Then she had asked him to join in.

And he had. He'd ripped off his dirty shirt, pushed his uniform pants down to his hips, and fucked her. Hard. Over and over, his cock pounding into her as she sucked the other guy off. He'd been disgusted. Sickened.

And so fucking turned on he'd come harder than he'd ever come before.

And then he kicked her out, barely giving her

enough time to collect the clothes she kept at his place before he ran to the bathroom and threw up.

All hopes of loving, committed relationships evaporated that day. Not because he loved her—he hadn't, not even close. Not because she cheated on him—although he was sure that probably played a small part, especially when he learned she'd been cheating on him from the very beginning.

It was the excitement he'd felt at watching. At being part of, even loosely, that unplanned threesome. How could he be turned on by watching someone else fuck his girlfriend? How could he be turned on by someone watching *him* fuck her?

No, it wasn't normal. It couldn't be. Which meant there must be something wrong with *him*. Something twisted and abnormal. So no, a normal relationship was out of the question. Just like a committed relationship was definitely out of the question—for him, at least. Which was fine, because he definitely didn't want to deal with the headache or the heartache.

So he had turned to the casual hook-up. Sex, just for the sake of sex. Wild and kinky or normal vanilla. He didn't care. It was just a means to an end and fun for everyone involved.

Which only made this odd obsession with Beth even more disconcerting. Well, that would end tonight—as soon as he found someone to hook-up with.

He read through some of the comments, his gaze scanning most of them and then dismissing them. A bored couple looking for a third party to spice up their sex life. One woman looking for someone to play with her new toys. Another woman looking for someone into bondage and submission.

Adam leaned closer to the screen, his brows lowered in thought. He hadn't tried anything like that yet. The closest he'd come to any bondage was tying one partner's hands to the headboard with a silk scarf while he wore a silicone cock ring. The knot hadn't held on the scarf and the ring had damn near cut off the circulation to his cock so the entire bondage play had lasted less than five minutes and left him swearing he'd never do anything like that again.

But maybe something that different was exactly what he needed. He moved the cursor over her name, still hesitating. Would he be able to let someone else tie him down? To totally submit and allow himself to be completely dominated?

His cock twitched in his lap. From excitement? He reached down, fisted his hand around the semi-hard length, and stroked. His eyes closed, imagining someone standing over him with long stocking-clad legs that ended in five-inch spike heels. Leather collar. Leather straps. A blindfold—

His cock sprang to life, rock hard. Thick, long, the tip already wet with precum. He smeared the thick drops along his shaft, his head tilted back as his hips thrust faster with each stroke. Fuck. Holy shit.

Yes. Definitely. He could definitely see himself submitting.

The image of the unknown dominatrix became clearer. Black leather garter belt, clean shaven pussy. Round hips and full breasts framed in leather bindings with a slender chain running from one nipple to the next.

His hand moved faster, his balls pulling tight as the chair rocked and bounced under his thrusting hips. Fuck, this felt so good. Would feel so much better with the dominatrix standing over him, a whip in her hand, trailing the leather strands over his chest and cock.

Adam leaned back even more, his ass hanging over the edge of the chair, the clenching of his fist around his cock almost painful as he jerked his wrist. Stroking harder. Faster.

His breathing turned to sharp gasps, the sound short and harsh to his own ears. His mind's eye traveled up the unknown woman's body, along the slender column of her neck to the thick fall of dark wavy hair that fell around her shoulders. To full lips parted in a teasing smile and hazel eyes glazed with need and passion.

Beth.

Release crashed over him, tearing a scream from his chest. Semen shot onto the flat planes of his abdomen, coated his clenched fist. Hot. Steamy. He kept stroking, harder, faster, his body convulsing with each stroke as he smeared the thick liquid across his stomach, his balls, his cock.

Beth.

He groaned her name, hips still bucking as the climax continued rolling over him.

Fuck. Holy fuck. God, yes.

Time stilled, his hand wrapped around his limp cock, warm with the stickiness of his body. He sucked in a deep breath, struggling to fill his lungs with air.

Fuck. When was the last time he'd had an orgasm like that? He frowned, trying to remember.

Never. Not even that day he'd walked in on his girlfriend and participated in his first threesome.

How would it feel to come like that inside a hot wet pussy? A shudder went through him at the thought. *That's* what he wanted to feel. Fuck yeah. He swallowed in anticipation. Yes, *that*. He wanted that.

He groaned and moved his hand away from his cock, reached down for the towel that had slid from his shoulder and wiped his hand, his stomach. His cock and balls and thighs. Christ, he didn't remember ever coming this much before.

But he would again. Soon. Very soon.

He tossed the towel to the side and straightened in the chair, his hand reaching for the mouse. The lonely dominatrix was still in the room, still looking for a partner for tonight.

Adam moved the mouse over her screen name, ready to click on it and send her a private message. His finger hovered over the mouse button, waiting.

Waiting for what? He shook his head, told himself to just do it. For fuck's sake, just do it.

But did he want her? Or just the experience?

Or was it the image of Beth that had ripped such pure pleasure from his body?

No—it was just the experience. He was reading too much into the wild imaginings of his mind. Just click on the unknown woman's name and set up a meeting. That was all he had to do.

His finger lowered to the mouse, resting on the button, a second away from clicking it. The computer dinged, the signal for a new arrival in the chatroom. Adam's gaze slid to the side pane, zeroing in on the latest arrival's screen name.

Lookin2B84Fun

His cock sprang to life and he sucked in a quick breath, one filled with disbelief and surprise.

And a searing flash of jealousy.

Beth.

Chapter Six

Nerves fluttered in her stomach, fast and heavy, growing even stronger as Beth stepped off the elevator and searched for the right room. It was ridiculous to feel so nervous. She was meeting Adam, not some random stranger.

Except Adam *was* a stranger. She'd only met him once before, three weeks ago. What did she really know about him? Well, other than that he was exceptionally talented in bed. Yes, they'd had sex. Lots of sweaty, toe-curling, screaming sex. That didn't mean she *knew* him.

And there had been something different about him this evening when he sent her a direct message. Something intense and almost needy in spite of the shortness of their messages. She'd been online barely a minute when he sent her a message.

Meet me?

Two simple words. She almost didn't answer. Not just because she hadn't heard from him the night before, although she had enough self-awareness to know that part of her was a little...hurt. Maybe that was why she hesitated—because she knew it was irrational to be hurt, knew that they meant nothing to each other.

It was sex. Just sex. Allowing any emotional attachment was dangerously insane.

So yes, she almost ignored it, thinking that maybe it would be smarter to find someone else. Only she didn't want someone else, and that scared her—scared her enough that she almost left the chatroom

And then he sent another message: *really want you tonight*.

A shiver danced across her skin as she recalled the words on the screen. It was so much more than desire and need. The words made her feel *wanted. Needed*. Beth hadn't felt that way in such a long time.

She couldn't remember the last time she'd felt that way. Ever.

So here she was, more nervous than she'd been the last time, questioning the wisdom and sanity of what she was about to do.

She glanced at the slip of paper in her hand then studied the room numbers as she walked along the hallway. The carpet was thick, making her ankles wobble in the four-inch heels that pinched her feet. Nervous sweat covered her palms and she brushed her hands along her skirt. Silly, so silly.

It was Adam. She shouldn't be so nervous.

She paused in front of the next door, double-checked the room number, then raised her hand to knock—and hesitated again. Tonight was a little different than their first night together. A different hotel, this one a little more than an hour away from her small apartment in York. No meeting in the hotel bar for drinks—this hotel just over the line in Maryland didn't have a bar. No meeting first for casual conversation. No small talk or even a semblance of getting to know each other first.

Well of course not. They'd already done that.

All she had to do was knock on the door.

Beth took a deep breath, trying to calm the increasing flutter of nerves in her stomach.

Just knock on the door.

That's all she had to do—just knock.

She took another deep breath then curled her fingers against her palm and rapped her knuckles against the door. Soft, the sound so quiet even she had trouble hearing it. There was no way Adam would be able to hear it, not from inside.

Except he must have because the door opened almost immediately.

Beth's heart slammed into her chest, the breath freezing in her lungs as she stared at Adam. He stood in front of her, a white towel wrapped low around his waist. The length of his cock, already hard, pushed against the material, making her wonder how the towel was staying in place. Her gaze traveled up his body, her mouth watering at the sight of flat sculpted abs and broad chest sprinkled with curly hair. Chiseled jaw, firmly set. Straight nose. Strong face. His thick hair was damp, as if he'd just gotten out of the shower, and slicked back off his forehead.

But it was his eyes that stole the breath from her lungs. Such a deep blue, the color almost black in the dim light surrounding him—and filled with such need, such passion.

Such determination.

Beth couldn't move, her body frozen in place as he stared at her with such ferocious intensity. Frozen?

How could she be frozen, when desire burned so hot inside her at that look he leveled on her? Need coiled inside her, tight and urgent, as wetness grew between her legs.

Part of her screamed, warning her to run away. He was dangerous. *This* was dangerous. This was Adam, but a different Adam. Intense, determined, ferocious.

She didn't want to run away, not when her body screamed for him. Not when need heated her blood and seared her skin.

But she couldn't move—not toward him, not away from him. She was paralyzed, unable to control any part of her body. Did Adam know? He must have, because he reached out and caught her hand, gently tugged until she was inside the room, the heat of his body burning her—and he wasn't even touching her except for her hand.

He closed the door, the click loud and somehow ominous in the darkened room. She must have jerked in surprise because his eyes met hers, his gaze holding her in place. He dropped her hand, trailed his fingers up her arm, across her shoulder to her throat. His touch was liquid fire, burning her as he placed his hand against the heavy pulse beating in her neck. His eyes darkened even more as he stepped closer and looked down at her.

"Are you afraid?"

Beth's lips parted but no words came out. Was she? Yes. No. She wasn't sure but she nodded anyway.

Adam's thumb swept across her lower lip, his deep eyes searching hers with that same intensity. "Don't be."

Then his mouth crashed against hers, his tongue sweeping in and tangling with hers. Hot. Seeking.

Demanding and possessing. She sighed and leaned into him, all fear and anxiety fleeing under his touch. This was so much more than a kiss. This was...she didn't know how to describe it, didn't know if words even existed to describe it. Carnal, yes. But more than that.

His hands roamed over, his fingers undoing the buttons of her silky blouse and spreading the sides wide. He growled, broke the kiss and pushed the blouse over her shoulders and down her arms. But he didn't remove it, simply pulled it behind her, imprisoning her arms against her back and holding her like that with one strong hand.

Strong, yet somehow gentle.

His gaze traveled across her body, rested on the swell of her breasts. He cupped one in his free hand, ran his thumb across the tightened peak straining against the lacy cup. His fingers curled over the edges and pulled, her breasts falling free of the material, their fullness pushed even higher over the wadded lace under them.

She heard him gasp, felt his hot breath against her flushed skin as he bent over and dipped his head. His mouth closed over one peak, pulled it into his mouth and sucked. Bit down with his teeth and laved the tip with his tongue.

Her breath rushed from her in a loud gasp. Her back arched, her body begging him for more. He didn't disappoint, his mouth and tongue and teeth drawing new responses from her body. Wetness pooled between her legs, liquid fire that spread like lava. She needed to move, to press her hips against him, to feel the hard ridges of his cock against her. But she couldn't, not with the way her arms were trapped behind her, not with the way her body was pinned to the wall by his.

A sigh of disappointment escaped her when Adam released her nipple. He ran his tongue between the deep valley of her breasts, flicked it against the sensitive flesh along the swell of each one.

"Do you like that?" His voice was thick, ragged. Filled with need. She nodded, unable to speak. He pressed his mouth against her neck, dragged it up to her ear. Kissing, licking. Biting. His free hand trailed along her side, pulling at her skirt until the material bunched around her hips. His hand dipped between her legs and she felt him smile.

"No underwear. Did you do that for me?"

She nodded, unable to speak, barely able to think. She gasped as he slid one finger inside her, her head falling back. He traced her ear with his tongue as his finger stroked her, gliding in and out of her.

"You're so fucking wet, Beth. So fucking tight. I want to feel your tight pussy wrapped around my cock. That's all I've been able to think about. Do you want that?"

Oh God, yes. But she couldn't speak, could barely breathe as her hips pushed forward. Seeking.

He ran his tongue around her ear, bit down on the lobe. Pain and pleasure mixed, caused the breath to rush from her lungs.

"I think you like that. I can feel your pussy getting wetter. So fucking wet." He pulled his finger from inside her, brought it to her mouth and ran the tip of it across her lower lip. "Do you feel how wet you are? How hot?"

Beth's lids fluttered open, her gaze meeting his. Dark, intense. Need and passion and desire. Her stomach clenched, her muscles pulling tight at the sudden power soaring through her. *She* had done this to him.

She dipped her head forward, closed her mouth over his finger, and licked the wetness from it. Her own wetness, thick and tangy. Her gaze held his as she sucked, excitement filling her at the way his eyes flared, at the way his pupils dilated with need.

"Fuck. So fucking hot."

She released his finger, ran her tongue over her lip as he watched. He moved his hand between her legs again, dipped his finger into her pussy, brought it back to her mouth.

Her eagerness surprised her. She'd never done anything like this before, had never considered doing anything like this before. But God, it was such a turn-on. Tasting herself on his finger, watching the feral excitement grow in his eyes as he watched.

He slid his finger inside her again, stroking deep before pulling it once more. But he didn't bring it to her mouth. She sighed in disappointment, the sound surprising her and bringing a small smile to his mouth. He ran his wet finger across her chest and around one nipple, her skin glistening in the dim light. She sighed, her body arching, her hands clenching the air behind her. She tried to move her arms, wanted to reach between her own legs and touch herself. Wanted to paint his own body as he was painting hers.

But he shook his head, that small smile still on his face, and tightened his hold on her wrists.

"Not yet. Not until you come." His free hand squeezed her breast, his thumb and forefinger pinching her nipple. Pulling, twisting.

"You have such beautiful breasts. So big and soft and firm. Do you know what else I want to do with them?" Beth shook her head, struggled to catch her breath as he ran his free hand down her body. He slid two fingers deep inside her, pressed the heel of his palm against her clit. His mouth was close to her ear, his breath hot against her skin, his voice rough.

"I want to slide my cock between your breasts. Want to watch as I cum all over that creamy skin. Want to watch you spread my hot juice all over you as I pinch those beautiful big nipples."

Her head fell back, a hoarse scream escaping her as her climax shattered over her. Adam plunged his fingers deeper, in and out, faster as her body clenched around them. Her hips bucked, her body convulsing, searching for more and trying to push away at the same time. It was too much. Too intense, this odd sensation of pleasure and pain. She heard his voice, disjointed words of encouragement and wonder as her climax grew. Rolling, shuddering. Pure fire exploding, need growing. Too much. Not enough. She needed more, needed less. She couldn't tell, didn't know, her mind shattering along with her body.

And then his hands disappeared, her arms were free. She reached out, blind, unable to see, needing something to hold onto, to anchor herself against the storm crashing into her.

His mouth was on her, his tongue sweeping across her clit as he spread her open with his fingers. Wider, wider still as his tongue slipped inside her. Tasting, licking, probing as her muscles clenched around him.

Another climax crashed over her, robbing her of thought, stealing her strength. Her legs buckled as a hoarse scream ripped from her throat. She was falling, hurtling through darkness and light. Then she was flying, her feet somehow off the ground. She reached down, her hands tangling in the thick waves of his hair, her back pressed against the wall as Adam arranged her legs over his shoulder.

Oh God, how—never before—she couldn't—

But she was. Over and over as he pressed his tongue deeper inside, his fingers spreading her even wider. She screamed again, struggled to draw breath, felt her body clench and squeeze and convulse as yet another wave washed over her.

Beth couldn't breathe, couldn't think. She could only hold onto him as her body shattered, breaking into a million pieces before floating away.

Chapter Seven

Stay out of the chatroom. It's dangerous.

The scissors slipped from her fingers and hit the floor, bounced off the mat and slid past her feet. Beth stared down at them, her mind not comprehending what had just happened. Sluggish, slow to react.

No, not sluggish. Distracted.

Oh God, she was so distracted, had been all week.

She waved Courtney away then bent down to retrieve the scissors, dropping them in the disinfectant solution and pulling out another pair. The girl in the chair didn't even look up, her attention riveted on the e-reader held so close to her face. Beth blew out a quick breath and ran a comb through the girl's wet hair, trying to focus on what she was doing.

How could she focus when all she kept thinking about was Adam? What he'd done to her, how he'd made her feel. Desirable. Wanted. Sexy.

Dirty.

God, the things they'd done. The things *she'd* done. Her skin tingled as memory after memory spun through her mind with dizzying speed. It was so much more than sex.

And yet, it was nothing *but* sex. Raunchy, wild, untamed—just like her body's reaction to every single touch, every whispered word. Had she known such feelings existed? Had she known her body was capable of such responses? No, never. And she wanted more, wanted to feel that way again.

But the mere thought terrified her.

What was she doing? Was she getting in over her head?

Or was she already there?

It's dangerous.

Adam had repeated those words several times, warning her that not everyone in the chatroom was who they pretended to be. She knew that already, had been leery of the whole thing for just that reason. But his eyes had been so intense, his gaze totally focused on her when he said it—and when he told her to call *him* if she needed anything.

Anything at all.

What scared her most of all was that she wanted to, had almost done just that so many times this past week. It went beyond *want*, beyond *need* even. It was like an addiction, her body craving her next fix, one that only Adam could provide.

Her body was reacting even now, simply by thinking about him—about what they'd done together. Her stomach clenched and dampness pooled between her legs, the ache growing until it became almost painful. She wanted to drop everything she was doing and run to the back, lock herself away and jam her hand down her pants. To rub her finger over her clit, hard and fast until the ache changed to shattering release.

But oh God, it terrified her. She'd never felt this way before, so hungry. Starving and needy. What had Adam done to her?

What had she done to herself?

She squeezed her eyes shut and took a deep breath, searching for a control she was very much afraid was out of her reach. Just a few more hours then she could leave. She just had to survive a few more hours.

Beth finished the girl's hair, drying it with a final flourish before leading her to the register. A broad smile creased the girl's face as she tilted her head from side to side, her new cut swinging freely around her face. She said something, watched Beth with an expectant gaze, like she was waiting for a response. Beth muttered a few words through lips that felt numb, went back to her station to clean up. There was nobody else waiting just now, no other appointments. She could go to the back, take a break, try to calm herself down.

How long had she been sitting there, staring at the same page of the magazine before Courtney took a seat across from her? She didn't know, had no way of knowing, not even when Courtney asked her a question.

Beth shook her head, tried to pretend she had been so engrossed in the magazine that she hadn't heard. But Courtney was her best friend, had known her too long to fall for the ploy. She leaned across the table, her delicate brows lowered in a frown, and studied Beth.

"Okay, so who is he?"

"What? Who?"

"Whoever has you so distracted. It's like you're not

even here."

"I'm not—I mean, nobody. It's—" Beth forced herself to stop talking, knowing she was only making things worse.

"In all the years I've known you, I have never seen you like this. So out with it. Who is he?"

Could she tell Courtney? God no. She'd never understand. Not about the chatroom, not about hooking up with a stranger for sex. Not about Adam and certainly not about the things they'd done, the things *she'd* done.

Was there anything she *could* tell Courtney? Maybe, if she stripped everything down to the most basic G-rated version—if such a thing even existed. And maybe talking about him would help put things in perspective—for her, at least.

She ran her finger along the corner of the magazine, fanning the page edges with the tip of her nail. Courtney was still watching her, waiting. Should Beth wave her question away and try to change the subject?

She took a deep breath, working up the courage to say...something. "I, uh, I kind of met someone."

"What? When? Why haven't you said anything before now?" Excitement glowed in Courtney's eyes, her genuine happiness reflected in the smile lighting her face. She leaned her arms on the table and leaned forward, her head tilted to the side. "You can't stop there! Tell me all about him. I need details."

Details. Yes, of course she'd want details. But what could Beth say? She didn't really know Adam, didn't know anything about him other than his voracious sexual appetite and the fact that he was ready, willing, and able to do *anything*.

And the fact that no man, ever, had elicited such responses from her body. That no man had made her want to do the things they'd done. But she couldn't tell Courtney any of that. Not just because her friend would freak if she did, but because it was too personal. Beth was having a hard enough time dealing with it herself—no way could she admit to the things she'd done out loud. To another person.

But surely there was *something* Beth could tell her about Adam. She frowned, thinking back over the brief conversations they'd had. Not *conversations*—it had just been one, the first night they'd met. And the very few times they'd texted back and forth.

"Well. His name is Adam." And oh God, she didn't even know his last name! Beth cleared her throat, pushed away from the table and pulled two bottles of water from the refrigerator. She passed one to Courtney then took her time untwisting the cap from her own before taking a long sip.

Yes, she was stalling. Could Courtney tell? Of course she could.

Beth capped the bottle and placed it on the table in front her, holding it between her hands as she stared at the label. Better to look at that than meet her friend's curious gaze.

"He's a firefighter in—" She paused, frowning, trying to remember. "In Baltimore County, somewhere. He has the most gorgeous blue eyes, deep and dark. And thick wavy hair, the kind you want to run your hands through. All different shades of blonde. He almost looks like one of those surfer boys you see in the magazines but trust me, he is definitely all man!"

Courtney's smile grew wider and she made a small humming sound of appreciation. "Sounds very nice.

How old is he? How did you guys meet?"

"Oh. Uh, he's a few years older than me." Maybe. "And we just, you know, kind of met."

"Well, if the look on your face means anything, he must be something special."

"*Special?*" Beth choked the word out. "No! No, not even close. We've only gone out twice and—"

"Maybe, but the expression on your face is saying you're interested in a lot more."

Beth laughed, a real laugh that didn't hide her disbelief *or* dismissal of Courtney's assertion. "Trust me, I am not interested in *more*. The only thing I'm interested in is his fire hose—and how well he uses it."

"Beth! I can't believe you said that."

Neither could she, not really. But it was the truth. At least, as close to the truth as she could tell Courtney. There was no way she could tell her best friend how she'd met Adam—or *why*. So yeah, in a way, that's all Beth really was interested in.

She just hadn't expected all the feelings and needs and desires that had been unlocked since meeting him. Had she known she had those buried inside her? No, not even close.

That scared her. Well, maybe not *scared*—but it definitely worried her. As long as she kept reminding herself that it was just sex, she should be okay.

Hot, sweaty, toe-curling sex, but sex just the same. Nothing more. She and Adam would do their thing and then they'd both move on. This wasn't a relationship, not even close. It was an *encounter*. Beth figured they'd meet maybe one or two more times and that would be it. Any more than that and she'd run the very real risk of letting emotions get in the way. She couldn't afford to let that happen.

And it wasn't happening now, no matter what Courtney thought she saw in Beth's face. Courtney just wanted to keep believing in the fairy tale of happily-ever-after, even after her son's father had disappeared from the picture while she was pregnant.

Beth didn't believe in fairy tales. And she certainly wasn't looking for a happily-ever-after. She just wanted to have fun.

And that's exactly what she was doing. When she was done with Adam, she'd find someone else. Simple as that.

"What's wrong?"

Beth looked up, noticed the frown of worry on Courtney's face. "Nothing. Why?"

"I don't know. You just got this look on your face."

"No I didn't."

"Yeah, you did." Courtney tilted her head to the side, her blonde hair falling over her shoulder with the motion. The frown deepened as she studied Beth. "Almost like you were sad about something."

Beth forced a laugh as she pushed away from the table. "You're seeing things."

"I don't think so—"

"Yes, you are. I have nothing to be sad about. I'm finally having fun, that's all that matters." She offered Courtney a bright smile, wondering if it was enough to fool her friend.

If it was enough to fool herself.

It should be, because Beth was telling the truth. She *was* having fun, finally free of the idiot she had been seeing for too long, finally free of the worry and self-doubt that he had created inside her.

She had every reason to smile and absolutely no

reason to be sad. None at all.

Except she couldn't shake the feeling that, when the time came, she was going to miss Adam.

And she wasn't entirely sure she would be comfortable hooking up with anyone else after him.

Chapter Eight

"Christ, this shit tastes like charcoal and lighter fluid." Adam tossed the burger back on the plate and reached for the bottle of water next to his elbow. The guys were making similar comments, all tossed in Jay's direction. Everyone except Jimmy, who couldn't hear anyone because he was sitting there with his earbuds in, listening to who-knew-what.

"Not my fault I picked the short straw to cook. Again." Jay frowned at his own burger then slowly pushed his plate away. "Okay, yeah, that's pretty bad."

"Don't even pretend you didn't do this on purpose. You're usually not this bad."

"Yeah, sure. I deliberately doused the burgers because I wanted to starve tonight." Jay shook his head and got up from the table, grabbed his plate and headed toward the trashcan. "Do you know how long it's been since I've used a charcoal grill? Why the hell didn't day shift fill the tank on the gas grill? You want to blame someone, blame them."

"Oh bullshit. It doesn't take a genius to figure out

you're not supposed to throw the burgers on until *after* the grill stops flaming." Dale grabbed his own plate and headed to the trash can, a scowl on his face. Adam bit back a laugh, remembering how much Dale had been looking forward to the meat. Apparently his girlfriend, Melanie, had been on a vegetarian kick the last month. They were already taking bets on how long it would be before Dale finally blew.

"When the hell does Pete get back from vacation, anyway?" Adam made his own way to the trash can as he asked the question. Their lieutenant was the one who normally did all the cooking on their shift. Every single one of them took it as some kind of betrayal that he had abandoned them and left them to fend for themselves while he was gone.

"Not soon enough."

"For shit's sake, would you guys stop whining? It's not like we're going to starve. We'll just order pizza or something." Mikey pushed her way around them and dumped her own plate into the trash can. "You're all acting like a bunch of babies. And you're giving me a headache so knock it off."

"What the hell crawled up your ass?"

"Yeah. You've been grumpy all shift. What the hell's up with that?"

Mikey spun on her heel and pinned Adam with one of her classic glares: head tilted to the side, brows lowered over narrowed green eyes, lips pursed like she'd just been forced to suck a down a whole lemon. She reached back, redid her ponytail, then gave him another glare.

"I told you, I'm PMSing."

"Oh bullshit. You used that excuse two tricks ago. Don't try to use it again."

A small smile teased her mouth but only for a second. "Yeah, well. You guys drive me to it. I feel like I'm working with a bunch of little boys with all the constant whining going on."

Everyone laughed, including Dave, who had been the straight-laced grumpy ass of the shift. At least until he hooked up with his girlfriend, CC, last year.

No, not *hooked up*. That was the absolute wrong phrase to use. That implied a casual encounter—and Adam was the only one on their shift into that kind of thing. Probably the only one in the station. Hell, probably their whole fucking battalion. Which was fine by him—he wasn't cut out for a relationship. He'd learned that lesson already—the hard way. And yeah, ha ha, pun intended. Everyone else on his shift could settle down and play house if they wanted. Whatever suited them was fine by Adam.

But that wasn't him. It never would be. He preferred the freedom of no-strings sex. Casual encounters. No expectations.

That suited him just fine.

He moved back to the table and started cleaning up the rest of their burnt dinner. Mikey and Jay were arguing over what kind of pizza to get. Dale was trying to convince Dave to take the medic unit to pick it up. And Jimmy was sitting there, totally oblivious to everything with his earbuds still in.

Just another night with his perfectly imperfect dysfunctional family.

Sometimes, it was enough to drive him insane.

Usually, when he was feeling this way, he'd disappear downstairs, get on his phone, and play around in the chatroom. Maybe schedule a hook-up for the following day. Only he didn't feel like doing that tonight. The whole idea left him feeling antsy and unsettled and he didn't know why.

Or maybe he did and was just afraid to admit it—because he wasn't sure what he'd do if he saw Beth on there again.

He tried to warn her away from the chatroom the last time they were together, nearly two weeks ago. It was dangerous, he'd told her. He hadn't lied—it *could* be dangerous. There was no way to tell who you were really talking with, no way to tell who or what you might encounter when meeting in person. The game was new to Beth and he didn't want her to put herself in a dangerous position.

At least, that's what he tried to tell himself, even if he had never worried about something like that before. To each his own, right?

Except he still didn't want to see Beth in the chatroom, didn't want her taking unnecessary risks. That's why he broke down and told her that if she was ever in the mood, to call him directly and he'd help her out. No matter when.

Because yeah, he was so fucking noble that way.

It didn't matter how many times he tried to convince himself otherwise, he knew it was more than a concern for her safety that had prompted him to issue the personal invitation. He'd never done that before, not with any of his previous hook-ups. Not even his favorite ones. So why Beth? What was it that was so different about her?

Sure, she possessed a certain refreshing innocence, something he'd never encountered before in spite of all the things they'd done their last two times together. She wasn't the most beautiful woman he'd been with, either. Yes, Beth was very attractive and pretty. Short with generous curves, a killer smile and those gorgeous eyes. God, he loved the way her eyes changed colors when they were together, going from smoky green to warm brown and all the shades in between. She was eager in bed, willing to learn new things. And she was a fast learner, too.

A grin spread across his face as memories—clear and vivid—swirled through his mind. Yes, she was definitely a fast learner.

But none of that should matter. None of that was enough for him to break his own rules and actually issue an invitation like that. At least, it shouldn't be. So why the fuck had he?

By his own rules, they had one more time together. Just one. Adam didn't see any of his hookups more than three times, period. That was a hard-and-fast rule. It kept things clean and fun. No strings, no matter what.

If he were smart, he'd get in touch with Beth and schedule that third hook-up and be done with it—except part of him was afraid to.

Afraid that third time wouldn't be enough, that he'd want a fourth and a fifth and—

"Hey, Romeo."

Something hit Adam in the shoulder, jerking him to the side. He frowned and straightened in the chair, then twisted to the side to see Dale standing over him. "What the hell?"

"We've been calling your name for five minutes. Are you deaf?"

"Whatever." Adam rubbed his shoulder and tried to push all thoughts of Beth from his mind.

"What do you want on your pizza?"

"I don't know. The usual, I guess."

Mikey plopped down in the chair across from him and shook her head, her ponytail swinging. "No. No onion or peppers. The kitchen will reek if you get that."

"Since when do you care?"

"Since just now. Get something else."

"What the hell is wrong with—"

"No, seriously. I mean it." She shook her head again, the frown on her face deepening. Everyone turned to look at her, varying degrees of confusion on their faces. Adam opened his mouth to say something only to be stopped by Jay's hand clamping down on his shoulder—hard.

Adam rolled his eyes and pushed Jay's hand away. "Fine, whatever. Pepperoni and mushroom then. I don't care."

Mikey looked up from the orders she was scribbling on a small notepad and offered him a lopsided grin. "Aw. Are we pouting now?"

"Kiss my ass."

"With as much as you've been around? No thanks. That thing needs to be sterilized first."

Adam ignored the laughter that greeted her words, tried to pretend they hadn't struck a sore spot. And what the hell was up with that? Shit like that had never bothered him before. "Funny. Real funny."

Dave yanked the earbuds from Jimmy's ears then looked over at them. "Would you guys just finish up so we can call the order in and go pick it up?"

"Don't rush me." Mikey made a few more notes on the pad then ripped off the top sheet and handed it back over her shoulder. Dave took it from her then frowned as he read over it. "Five pizzas? There's only six of us."

"Yeah, and everyone wants something different.

Deal with it."

Dave muttered something under his breath and started to shove the small slip of paper into his pocket. The alarm went off, echoing around them. All movement stilled as the radio blared to life for a medic call—a car accident a few miles from the station.

Dave removed the note from his pocket and tossed it toward Mikey. "Looks like you guys are picking it up now."

Dave and Jimmy were hurrying from the kitchen when the alarm went off again, this time for the engine. The accident was now being dispatched as an auto fire with people trapped.

"Fuck."

"So much for dinner."

The room erupted in action, everyone running for the engine room. Less than a minute later, they were pulling out the door, sirens wailing and air horn blasting as Dale turned the hulking engine into traffic.

Adam slid his arms into the strap of the bottle hooked to the seat, glanced over the engine compartment to see Mikey doing the same. The air horn blasted again, long and loud as they approached an intersection, stopping long enough to make sure traffic was clear before going through it.

Thirty minutes later, they were back at the station, gathered around the large round table with open pizza boxes scattered in front of them. The auto fire with rescue had turned into a dud, called in by a concerned yet overreacting bystander when they noticed "smoke" coming from the hood of the car. The smoke had been nothing more than steam, and the rescue had been a simple case of the driver unlocking his door. The accident had been a simple fender bender with property damage only and they had cleared the scene within five minutes of their arrival. Even the medic crew had lucked out because neither driver wanted—or needed—to go to the hospital.

Adam reached for his third slice of pizza then scooped up the glob of cheese and pepperoni stuck to the box before Jay could get it. He shrugged and offered Jay an unapologetic grin. "Hey, it came off *my* slice. I have dibs."

"That doesn't—"

"Oh God, don't start. Please. You guys are like a bunch of babies." Mikey grabbed a slice of pizza and tossed it onto Jay's plate. "There. Now you can pull all the toppings from that. Better?"

"That's not—"

"Whatever." Mikey cut Jay off with a quick wave of her hand. "Now let's talk about Saturday night instead."

"What's Saturday night?"

"Nick is playing at Duffy's. What else?" Mikey wiped her mouth with a napkin and pushed away from the table. "Who all's going?"

There was a chorus of answers, all in the affirmative—which shouldn't have surprised Mikey. Their entire shift always went to Duffy's when Nick's band was playing. Even when he wasn't playing, they still went. Duffy's was their hangout.

"Is everyone bringing dates?" Jay looked around the table, like he didn't already know the answer.

"Of course. Well, everyone except Jimmy and Adam." Mikey answered the question with a roll of her eyes.

Jimmy leaned across the table to grab one of the pizza boxes and pulled it closer to him. "Nope, just

Adam. I'll actually have a date with me."

Silence greeted Jimmy's statement. He paused with the slice halfway to his mouth then lowered it and looked around. "What? Why's everyone staring at me?"

"You're bringing a date?" Adam didn't bother hiding his surprise—the same surprise everyone else had. But it wasn't just surprise he was feeling: a sense of something very much like dread filled him.

"Yeah, I am. Why is that so surprising?"

"Why? Because you and Adam are the confirmed bachelors, that's why. How the hell did you manage to snag a date?"

Jimmy opened his mouth to reply but Dave beat him to it. "Don't be too impressed. Sheila, one of the ER nurses, finally took pity on him and said yes. It's a mercy date, that's all."

"Why do you have to say things like that? It's not a mercy date." Jimmy took a huge bite of pizza, chewed and swallowed, then gave everyone a big grin. "She finally succumbed to my irresistible charm."

"Yeah. Not to mention your good manners." Mikey wadded a paper towel and threw it at him, which only made everyone laugh even harder.

"I guess that leaves our resident Romeo, huh?" Jay nudged Adam in the side. "Guess you'll be the odd man out."

"No, I can bring a date." Adam nearly choked on the words. What the hell was he saying? He didn't bring dates to shift outings, ever. The guys knew that—which was probably why they were all staring at him. He cleared his throat, wondering if the heat he felt spreading across his face was merely his imagination. "I just don't want to, that's all."

"Don't want to—or *can't?*"

"I think Adam could find all the dates he wanted. Isn't that right?" Dale gave him a knowing look, a hundred different meanings contained in the seconds-long glance. Adam clenched his jaw and wished to hell he had never mentioned his hook-ups to anyone. He was ready to say something to Dale—something along the lines of *go to hell*—but Mikey talked right over him.

"Then it's settled. A cook-out for twelve at our place in the afternoon then we'll all head to Duffy's."

The heat evaporated from Adam's face, replaced with a chill he didn't want to acknowledge. "I didn't say—"

But Mikey kept on talking, ignoring his lame attempts to get the words out of his mouth. No, he wasn't bringing anyone. Why would any of them think he would? But he couldn't get the words out, couldn't speak around the lump of dread clogging his throat.

It didn't matter because everyone was talking again, discussing if it was too late in the year for a cook-out despite the nice weather. Discussing if they wanted to do steaks and chicken or burgers and dogs. Warning Jay that he wasn't allowed to get near the grill.

The voices faded away, disappearing in the loud buzzing echoing in Adam's mind. Fuck. He didn't *want* to bring a date. Why the hell would they expect him to? They knew better, every single one of them.

Well, screw them. He didn't *have* to bring a date, and he sure as hell didn't have to explain why. And he was positive that not a single one of them would be surprised when he showed up solo—because that's what he did.

Always.

Chapter Nine

Beth leaned forward and adjusted the car vent so the cool air blew into her face. It wasn't hot out, not really—the bright blue sky was clear overhead, the air crisp and clean and carrying the scent of early autumn in spite of the mild temperature. In a few hours, when the sun sank below the horizon, it would be chilly enough to put on the light jacket folded on the seat next to her.

None of that mattered, not when she was sitting in the front seat of her car, sweat beading on her brow and coating her palms. The sweat had nothing to do with the mild temperature or bright sun and everything to do with nerves.

A lot of nerves.

They fluttered in her stomach, creating a huge ball of anxiety that grew larger with each passing minute. Beth tightened her hands on the steering wheel and leaned closer to the vent, sucking in a lungful of cooled air.

It didn't help, not that she thought it would. But

she was desperate, which meant she'd try almost anything if it meant calming her nerves.

Anything except putting her old car in gear and pulling out of the parking lot.

She was supposed to be meeting Adam here, at the Park-and-Ride in Maryland Line just off I-83. Not for sex—especially not in broad daylight. Especially not here, in full view of anyone passing by.

No, they were meeting for a—God, she was afraid to even think the word—date. A real, actual *date*, one that involved going out. Together. In public.

And not just *in public*, but to a cookout or party or something with people he worked with.

Beth still couldn't believe it, still didn't understand *why*. Maybe she was just overthinking it, giving the whole surreal thing more importance than it deserved. Adam had called the other night and said he needed a date for a shift outing, whatever that was.

No, she knew what it was. Now, at least. His shift—the guys he worked with—were getting together and everyone else was bringing a date. Adam said he didn't want to be the only solo guy there, so he invited her.

Her.

Beth still couldn't believe it. And she couldn't stop wondering *why*. Adam must certainly have his pick of lots of women. So why did he ask her? That's what she couldn't figure out.

Unless he just drew a random name from his long list of contacts. Yeah, that must be what happened. The more Beth thought about it, the more it made sense.

Because she couldn't think of any other reason why he would have called her.

Just like she didn't really understand why she had said yes. She shouldn't have. This was too dangerous, too much like the real thing. Beth wasn't sure if she wanted the real thing—with anyone. Not after her last disastrous relationship. She could handle the hook-up—at least, that's what she told herself. That was nothing more than casual sex. No strings, no expectations, no commitment. But to actually go *out*? On a date?

That was something else totally different.

And yet, she had agreed to it. That was what worried her the most. No, that wasn't right. What worried her the most was that she was actually looking forward to it. And *that* was dangerous. There could be no future with Adam. Thinking there might be, even only fantasizing about it, would only lead to one place: heartbreak.

Beth didn't want to go through that again.

A white SUV pulled into the parking lot, the tinted windows dark enough that she couldn't see the driver. Was it Adam, or someone else? She leaned closer, her pulse racing as the driver's side window slowly slid down to reveal a strong profile topped with thick blonde hair.

Her pulse sped up. Heat shot through her body and her skin flushed, turning warm and prickly. This was the first time she had seen Adam in full daylight and oh, what a sight it was.

Yes, she was definitely in trouble. Big time trouble.

The SUV stopped next to her car, the passenger side window sliding down. Adam leaned over, a wide smile on his face as he looked at her and said something. Her own window was up so she couldn't make out the words. Even if she could, she wasn't sure she'd be able to understand them, not when her mind was totally short-circuiting.

She pulled in one more deep breath, filling her lungs with cool air, then turned off the engine and tossed her keys into the large bag that doubled as a purse. Her hands were trembling, the palms damp with sweat. From nerves?

Or excitement?

It didn't matter because the result was the same.

Beth grabbed her bag and jacket and climbed out of the car, making sure the door was locked before closing it. One more deep breath to steady herself, then she opened the door of Adam's SUV and climbed in.

Or she tried to, anyway. The SUV sat higher than she realized. Thank goodness there was a sidestep attached or else she really would have had to climb up.

"Need a hand?"

"No, I'm good." Beth grabbed the handhold attached to the inner door frame then did a quick bounce, practically jumping into the passenger seat. The long skirt twisted around her legs and she had to shift to readjust it. Heat filled her face as she smoothed the material across her thighs. So much for impressing him with her grace and coordination.

She shifted once more then turned to face Adam, ready to make a joke or comment about short people problems. The words died in her throat as Adam's mouth closed over hers. Hot, eager, possessing.

A soft moan escaped her and she leaned into the kiss. Her hand curled against his chest, her fingers twisting in the soft material of his shirt. The urge to climb over the console and straddle him was instant, almost as urgent as the need that suddenly coursed through her body. But Adam broke the kiss and pulled away before she could do anything.

"You look nice."

Beth looked down at the loose shirt and full-length skirt she had on. Casual and cool, not too fancy but not sloppy, either. She smoothed the material over her legs once more then glanced over at Adam. He was wearing faded jeans that hugged his legs and a dark blue t-shirt that pulled tight across his broad chest.

"Thank you. It's, uh, not too dressy, is it?"

"Nope. It's perfect." His mouth curled into a lopsided grin then he shifted in the seat and eased the SUV out of the parking lot. Silence settled between them as they drove south on I-83, stretching to the point where Beth grew uncomfortable.

She stole a glance at Adam from the corner of her eye. His left arm rested on the door frame, his right hand curled loosely around the steering wheel as he guided the SUV along the interstate. He looked relaxed. Confident. At ease.

So maybe she was the only one uncomfortable. But how could she *not* be? This was only their third time meeting—and the first time outside of a hotel room. They hadn't needed to talk the other times. No words had been necessary, not outside of the dirty talk while they were having sex.

Beth shifted in the seat, her mind searching for something—anything—to say. She gently cleared her throat then looked over at Adam once more.

"You, uh, said this is a get-together with your shift?"

"Yeah. Nothing fancy, just a quick cookout at Mikey and Nick's place before we head to Duffy's. Nick's band is playing there tonight."

Beth nodded as if she knew exactly who he was

talking about. She didn't, of course. "Mikey and Nick. Are they, uh, a couple?"

"Yeah—one with a long history. Recently reunited, though. We're still waiting to see how long it takes before they finally tie the knot."

"Oh. That would be nice. I'm so happy it's legal now."

Adam looked over, a frown creasing his forehead. "What's legal?"

"Getting married."

"Why wouldn't it be?"

"Well, you know, because people are so small-minded and everything."

"I'm not following you."

Now it was Beth's turn to frown. "Gay marriage? You just said that your friends were going to get married and I—"

Adam's laughter cut her off. The sound, deep and warm, washed over her. It was a nice laugh, honest and light. Maybe even a little teasing. Embarrassment heated her face—not because he was laughing *at* her, she was fairly certain he wasn't. The laugh didn't have that biting edge to it that she had grown so accustomed to. But she was still embarrassed because it was obvious she had said something wrong to cause the laughter.

Adam shook his head, a broad smile still on his face as he reached over and grabbed her hand. He brought it to his mouth and pressed a quick kiss to her knuckles, then threaded his fingers with hers and rested their joined hands on the center console.

"They're not gay. Mikey is a girl. A firefighter on our shift."

"Oh. I thought…never mind. I'm so sorry. I didn't

mean—"

"Not a big deal. It happens a lot. Her real name is Michaela. Nick calls her Kayla, but the rest of us call her Mikey."

Beth nodded and looked away, wondering if her face was still red. Probably. How could she be so stupid? She should have never opened her mouth, should have never said anything.

Should have never agreed to accompany Adam today. What if she said the wrong thing when she met his co-workers? What if she did something to embarrass him? She didn't want that to happen, didn't want to see undisguised impatience and biting condemnation in Adam's blue eyes as he laughed at her. She didn't think she could handle that. No, they weren't together. Not even close. But she didn't want anything to tarnish the memories of the two times they *had* been together. She wanted to keep those memories close, wanted to be able to pull them out on lonely nights and recall them with fondness, not with embarrassment and regret.

Today was a mistake. Agreeing to go with Adam was a mistake. She should have left well enough alone. It was one thing to meet for sex—she could handle that. At least, that's what she kept telling herself. She wasn't so sure anymore. But this? Spending the day with Adam, meeting his co-workers? It was too much like a date. Too much like the beginning of a...a *relationship*.

She should tell him she changed her mind. Ask him to take her back—

"You okay over there?"

"Hm?" She jumped a little, startled by his voice. "Yeah. Um, actually, I was thinking—"

"Thanks again for coming with me today. I've been looking forward to it."

Beth's mouth snapped shut and she squirmed against the sudden heat flaring inside her. Had he chosen the words deliberately? *Coming with me.* And oh God, how could three little words create such an extreme reaction in her? Excitement danced in her stomach and damp heat grew between her legs.

And then the rest of his words registered. He had been looking forward to it? Really? Did he mean it, or was he just saying it to be nice?

And why did she have to second-guess everything? Beth had sworn she wouldn't do that anymore. She had promised herself that she was going to distance herself from the past, that she wasn't going to let her ex's constant negativity influence her. No more doubting herself. This was supposed to be the *new* her.

So she'd go with Adam and enjoy herself. Just spend the day with him and try to relax and have fun and not read too much into it. She squeezed his hand and offered him a small smile.

"I've been looking forward to it, too." Beth's gaze drifted to the passing scenery, taking in the colors of the leaves on the trees flanking the interstate. They were just starting to turn, reds and oranges, scattered here and there among the green. Just another reminder that Fall was here, in spite of the warmer temperatures. This was her favorite season, a time where nature shed its summer cloak and started the wait for its rebirth in the Spring. Was that what she was doing? Shedding her old self, searching, waiting?

Maybe. Or maybe she was just being melodramatic today.

"So how many people are on your shift? Where's your station? Do you have one of those great work schedules where you're off for months at a time?"

Adam laughed again and tossed a quick glance in her direction. "For months at a time? Don't I wish. No, it doesn't quite work that way. We work two ten-hour days, two fourteen-hour nights, then we're off for four."

"Fourteen hours? I can't imagine working that many hours straight."

"It's not too bad, unless we run all night. We've been lucky the last few tricks and haven't had much after midnight. The station backs up to the interstate as you head into the city, so we tend to get a lot of accidents, things like that."

"Doesn't that get...I don't know—depressing or something? How do you deal with it?"

Adam shrugged as a grin teased the corners of his mouth. "You just get used to it. It's part of the job, you know?"

No, she didn't, but she figured he probably already guessed that.

"As for how many guys are on my shift—right now, we have seven. Dave and Jimmy are on the medic unit and there's five of us on the engine. Dale's the driver, Pete is our lieutenant, then there's Mikey, Jay, and me. We have a vacancy for Captain—the last guy we had was an asshole and they haven't transferred anyone in since he left. They're also talking about adding a second engine to our house but who knows if it'll ever happen. You'll get a chance to meet everyone except Pete, because he's on vacation right now."

Beth nodded. She repeated all the names in her head, wondering if she'd end up forgetting by the time they got to wherever they were going. Nerves fluttered in her stomach again and she ruthlessly pushed them away. It was normal to be nervous, she told herself. No reason to let the nerves take control.

Adam merged the SUV off the interstate and onto the Baltimore beltway. Traffic was heavier now but it didn't matter because they weren't on the beltway for long. Ten minutes later, Adam was guiding the SUV into a residential neighborhood and parking along the curb in front of an attractive split-level house. The front yard was neatly manicured, the walkway leading to the door bordered by dormant flower beds. Two large pots of colorful mums sat on either side of the porch, along with a comical scarecrow.

"So this is Mikey's house?"

"Actually, it's Nick's. Mikey was living in a renovated barn until they got back together." Adam turned the engine off then got out, pocketing his keys as he walked around to her side. Beth opened the door, frowning as she tried to figure out the best way to climb down without falling on her face. It was a misplaced worry because Adam was suddenly right next to her, lifting her out. His arms wrapped around her as her body slid down his, all hard muscle and masculine heat. A little groan escaped her when he pulled her closer and claimed her mouth with his.

The kiss was slow. Deep. Thorough. Like he couldn't get enough of her. She sighed and wrapped her arms around his neck, giving in to the velvety slide of his tongue against hers. Needing more, forgetting where they were—

Until a teasing voice called out.

"There's a spare room in the basement if you need it."

Adam eased his mouth from hers, a grin curling one corner of his full mouth as he slowly stepped away. He looked over his shoulder, the grin blossoming into a full smile.

"Bite me, Mikey." He reached for Beth's hand and gave it a tug. "Come on. I'll introduce you to the guys."

Chapter Ten

Duffy's was packed as usual. Nick's band always drew a crowd, which was why Grant—the owner of Duffy's—had them here at least once a month. Adam preferred the other nights, when the floor space was dominated by two pool tables instead of a teeming throng of sweaty bodies. Like everyone else on his shift, he preferred a smaller crowd, one where you didn't have to scream to be heard.

But they still tried to get here whenever Nick was playing, as long as their shift wasn't working. To support Nick—and because Mikey always guilted them into it. Yet for all the times they'd been here, this was the first night every single one of them brought a date along.

Adam reached for the plastic cup of beer and brought it to his mouth. He took a long swallow, his gaze scanning the bodies bunched together on the crowded dance floor. Beth was out there, dancing to an old rock song with Melanie and CC. A bright smile wreathed her flushed face as she moved to the beat of the music.

Adam still couldn't believe he'd asked her along tonight. No, it was more than that. Once he decided to ask her, he'd actually been looking forward to it. For the first hour at the cookout, Beth had been quiet and reserved, her discomfort obvious. She'd slowly come out of her shell, relaxing enough to join in the conversation. He had even coaxed her into playing some cornhole and they had managed to come in second place in the impromptu tournament that Mikey had devised. Adam's gaze drifted to the loose blouse Beth was wearing. Even from here, he could still see the silly button she was wearing: a big white round one, with the number 2 scrawled on it. The top of the two had been drawn as a comical smiley face.

Apparently, Mikey had raided Nick's school supplies before the cookout.

Adam lowered his cup to the table then glanced down at the matching button on his own shirt. He frowned then reached up and took it off, tossing it on the table. It slid across the surface and came to a stop in a small puddle of beer near one of the pitchers.

What the fuck was he doing? Bringing a date to a shift party? Playing games and wearing stupid winner buttons? What the hell was wrong with him? He needed to have his fucking head examined. What made it worse was the fact that he'd actually been enjoying himself. Beth was fun to be around once she got over her nervousness and shyness. She had an open laugh and an easygoing smile that drew everyone in. Well of course she did. She was a hairdresser, she interacted with people all the time. Being open was probably part of her job, kind of like a bartender was always so good at listening.

Adam's gaze slid to the bar, coming to rest on Jay and his girlfriend, Angie. She still worked here at Duffy's one or two nights a week, despite her new job as a veterinarian. And on the nights that Nick's band played, Jay usually jumped behind the bar with her to help out.

Just one big happy couple.

Like Mikey and Nick. And Dave and CC. And Dale and Melanie. Christ, it was enough to make his gut clench in disgust. And here he was, playing right along with the whole game.

With Beth.

With a woman he'd picked up online for the sole purpose of getting laid.

Yeah, he needed his fucking head examined—especially because he'd actually been enjoying himself.

He grunted, calling himself a fool as he reached for his cup again. Something kicked his foot and he looked up, surprised to see Dave studying him from across the table.

"Why do you look so pissed?"

Adam could barely hear the other man even if he didn't have trouble making out the words. That didn't mean he wanted to answer, not when he'd have to shout.

Not when he didn't really have an answer to give.

He shook his head and brought one finger to his ear, silently telling the paramedic he couldn't hear. Apparently, that excuse wasn't going to work because Dave stood up and walked around the table then lowered himself into the empty chair next to Adam.

"So, what's going on?"

"Nothing, why?"

"Then why do you look so pissed off?"

"I'm not."

Dave studied him for several long seconds then shook his head and turned to look out over the dance floor. Another minute went by before he turned back to Adam with a small smile. "Beth seems nice."

"She is." Probably too nice, especially for someone like him. Adam expected Dave to make a similar joke but he didn't.

"So where'd you meet her?"

"Uh, online." In a chatroom for hook-ups. No way in hell was he going to tell Dave that, though. Let him think Adam was talking about online dating or something as equally ridiculous.

"How long have you guys been seeing each other?"

"We haven't—" Adam stopped, took a quick swallow of beer, stared down into the cup. "I mean, not long. This is only our, uh, third time out."

Yeah. Third time. Three home runs and the game was over. Tonight would be the last time he saw Beth. He had rules for a reason, and no way in hell was he going to break them—no matter how much fun he was having with her tonight.

And if tonight was going to be his last time with her, what the hell was he doing sitting here, talking to Dave? He should be with Beth, somewhere private and quiet with his dick planted solidly in her tight wet pussy.

And fuck, instant hard on, just like that. Except it wasn't *just like that*, not when he'd been fighting it all day, ever since he picked her up earlier. Yeah, it was time for them to leave. He would take her back to her car. The park-and-ride area was secluded. He could save some money on another hotel room by making use of the big back seat of his SUV. Then they'd part ways and that would be that.

The song ended, loud applause and cheers filling the silence following the final chord. Another song started up almost immediately, this one an eighties rock ballad.

Adam drained his beer then pushed away from the table. Beth and Melanie and CC were walking toward him, laughing and breathless. He swallowed past the sudden lump in his throat, wondering why the hell it felt like something just punched him square in the gut when Beth's gaze met his.

Probably the damn burgers he'd chowed down on earlier.

He ignored the inner voice that called him a liar and grabbed Beth's hand, leading her back out onto the dance floor. She stepped into his arms with no hesitation, her head tilted back as she looked up at him. Adam ran one hand down along her back, lower to the full roundness of her ass. He pulled her even closer, fitting her hips against him, the hard length of his erection pushing against her stomach.

Her eyes flared with instant heat and she quickly looked away. Her tongue darted out and swept across her lower lip before pulling it between her teeth. Adam groaned then leaned forward, pressed his mouth against her ear.

"I want to watch you do that to my cock. Want to watch as your tongue swirls around the head, licking me. Sucking me."

Tremors raced through Beth's body as she stumbled against him. Adam pulled back, just enough to look down at her. A smile crossed his face when he saw the blush fanning across her cheeks. Her eyes closed, the lashes dark crescents against her flushed skin. Adam leaned down and pressed a kiss against the pulse beating against the tender flesh of her throat. Another tremor shook her when he dragged his mouth along her neck and gently bit down on the lobe of her ear.

"I want to dip my hand under your skirt and play with that beautiful clit of yours. Dip my fingers deep inside that tight little pussy and feel how wet you are. Want to taste you on my fingers. Right here, with everyone watching."

Beth's eyes flew open, horror and excitement mingling on her face. She looked around, no doubt to see if anyone was listening, then quickly shook her head.

"I don't—"

"I'm only teasing. About doing it right here, I mean. But I absolutely do want to do all that. And more. So much more." Adam pressed a quick kiss against her mouth, hard and fast, then stepped back. "Are you ready to leave? Go have some private fun?"

For a horrifying second, Adam honestly thought she was going to say no. But it must have just been his imagination because she finally nodded, that full lower lip still pulled between her teeth.

He wrapped his hand around hers and moved through the crowd back to their table so she could get her bag. A few quick goodbyes—quick enough that he knew he'd get the third degree come day shift—and then he was leading Beth back across the dance floor, this time toward the door.

He helped her into the front seat, watching as she smoothed the material of her skirt around her thighs. Fuck, he couldn't wait. He needed a taste, just a quick taste.

Adam leaned in, dipped his hand under the hem of the skirt and up along her bare leg. Smooth flesh, warm and soft. Up higher to her inner thigh, higher still—

Beth stiffened, her legs swiftly closing. "Adam, what—"

"Sh. I need to feel you. Need to see how wet you are."

"We're in the parking lot—"

"Nobody can see." He caught her gaze with his, held it, let her see how much he wanted this. She released a heavy sigh, the sound almost a low moan, and eased her legs apart.

Adam dragged his hand higher along her thigh, his knuckles brushing against the lace of what he knew was her thong. He stroked her through the damp material. Once, twice, her hips rising to meet each stroke.

He eased the material to the side, baring her pussy to his touch. And fuck, she was so wet. So fucking hot. He flicked the hard flesh of her clit, heard her moan as her hips surged toward his touch.

She reached for him, her fingers tangling in his hair as he kept stroking. Her hips lifted once more, silently begging with each thrust, with each harsh gasp that escaped her. Adam swallowed back his own groan and slid two fingers inside her. Muscles clamped around them, hot and wet and so fucking tight. He reached down with his free hand and rubbed the hard length of his cock through the denim of his jeans as he pumped his fingers into her tight pussy.

"Fuck, Beth. You are so fucking hot. Do you have any idea how fucking hot this is? How much I want to see you come right here?"

She muttered something, the words unintelligible. She grabbed her skirt with both hands, yanked it up past her hips, exposing her bare wet pussy. Her back arched and her hips lifted off the seat as his fingers slid into her. Harder. Faster. Deeper.

Adam glanced over his shoulder to make sure there was nobody else in the parking lot. Even if there was, they wouldn't be able to see anything. Not much, anyway, since he was parked in the far corner.

He turned back, his gaze dropping to his hand, watching his fingers disappear into Beth's tight heat. It wasn't enough. He wanted more. So much more.

He tore at the button of his jeans and struggled one-handed with the zipper. His cock sprung free, hard and thick and long. Eager, twitching with anticipation. He wrapped his hand around himself and stroked, hard, almost painfully as his gaze rested on Beth's pussy. Wet, so wet, glistening in the overhead light of the SUV.

Adam leaned closer, bent his head down and ran his tongue across her clit. Beth moaned, a breathy sigh that made his cock jump with excitement.

"Hold yourself open, Beth. I want to watch you come. Spread that pussy for me."

Adam held his breath, waiting to see if she'd do it for him. For all he knew, she hadn't even heard him. Fuck, he wasn't even sure he'd said the words out loud. His focus was centered on watching his fingers slide in and out of her, on stroking his own cock at the same time.

Her hands moved, slowly slid down to her lap. She hesitated, slid them closer to her own pussy. And then yes, fuck yes, she was parting her lips with her fingers, stretching, spreading herself apart, exposing damp pink flesh to his eyes.

"Fuck. Beth. God, yes." He eased his fingers from her wet pussy, dragged them across his cock, then slid them back inside her. Three this time, spreading, stretching. In and out as her back arched even more. A strangled cry caught in her throat as her body tensed, froze...then shook with the intensity of her climax. Her pussy clenched around his fingers, squeezing, over and over and over. Words fell from her mouth, too soft and fast for him to understand. And fuck, he didn't care, not when his balls were drawing tight, not when his own body felt like it was turning inside out.

Her orgasm eased, her breathing still harsh but not as desperate. Adam moved his dripping fingers from her pussy and wrapped them around his cock, spreading her silky wetness along the hard length. He stroked harder, faster, waiting for his own orgasm to crash over him.

"Watch me, Beth. Watch me come." It was an order, a rough growl that demanded and begged all in one breath. He felt her shift on the seat, sensed her eyes on him as he kept stroking.

Hard. Fast. Faster.

His head fell back on a low growl as his climax surged through him. Intense, powerful. He forced his eyes open, looked down as he kept stroking. Semen, thick and milky, spurted from his cock onto the gravel parking lot. He groaned, ran his palm across the tip of his cock, spread the cum over the length. Hot, sticky.

"Fuck." He released the hold on his cock and leaned against the door, his chest heaving with each harsh breath. "Fuck. That was definitely different."

Beth shifted beside him. He turned, saw her struggling to pull her skirt back into place. A bright flush colored her cheeks, the red clearly visible in the overhead light as she focused on something to her left.

Yeah, that had definitely been different.

And probably something Beth had never even considered doing. What the fuck was wrong with him? Getting Beth off by finger fucking her in the front seat of his SUV? With the door wide open, so anyone walking by could see? Jerking off while standing next to his car, in full view of anyone who happened to venture outside?

Was this a new fucking low for him? Or had he become so fucking warped that this was his normal?

And fuck, he was growing hard again just thinking about what they'd just done—what *he'd* just done. He bit back an oath and ran both hands down the front of his jeans, then shoved his cock back into his pants. He needed to take Beth back to her car then go home, put tonight behind him.

Except he couldn't. Not yet. He didn't want to drop Beth off anywhere. He wanted—*needed*—to feel her tight pussy clamp around him one more time. Just one more time, that was all.

He just didn't know if she wanted the same thing, not when she was sitting there, very obviously looking away from him.

Adam leaned in, ran a hand up her arm and let it rest on her shoulder. She stiffened for a brief second then slowly turned toward him. Her eyes didn't meet his, though.

"You okay?"

"Yeah. Fine."

"You don't sound it." He traced one finger along her jaw, dipped it under her chin and tilted her head up so she was looking at him. His eyes searched hers, trying to figure out what she was thinking. What she was feeling.

He leaned in, caught her mouth with his. The kiss was gentle, reassuring, with just enough pressure to allow her to pull away if she wanted.

She didn't.

Adam gave a silent prayer of thanks then ended the kiss. Wide eyes, their color a mix of green and gold and brown, stared back at him. "You sure you're okay?"

Beth hesitated then slowly nodded, her gaze slipping away from his. "I've never—I haven't done anything like that before."

"Neither have I." He pressed another kiss to her mouth, this one lingering. Her body softened, leaned toward his own as a soft sigh escaped her. Christ, much more and he'd be ready for round two, right here in the parking lot again.

Adam pulled away, his gaze holding hers. "Feel like going someplace a little more private?"

"Like where?"

It was on the tip of his tongue to say a hotel. It was the only place that made sense. He didn't want to fuck Beth in the back seat, not after what they'd just done in the parking lot. This was their last time together, he could spring for another night in a hotel room. She deserved at least that much.

Which was why he nearly choked when the unexpected words finally fell from his lips: "My place."

Chapter Eleven

It was a bachelor pad. Neatly kept and mostly clean, but still a bachelor pad. Beth stood in the middle of the room, her shoulders hunched around her ears, and looked around as Adam moved past her, turning on lights. Leather sofa and matching recliner. A wooden coffee table and matching end tables. Each end table held a single plain lamp and nothing else. Magazines were scattered across the surface of the coffee table, along with a thick text book opened in the middle. A pad of paper with scrawled notes sat next to the heavy book.

The walls were bare except for the large screen television, neatly placed in the center above a low shelf with more electronic equipment. The far wall of the living room opened into a pass-through window leading to the kitchen. Two stools were shoved under the overhang of the counter. A loaf of bread and a bag of pretzels sat next to a coffee cup in the middle of the counter.

A small dining nook was off to her left, complete

with a round wooden table and four matching chairs. A dark hallway stretched out beyond the dining nook, no doubt leading to—

She didn't need to think about where it led. Not right now.

So she focused on what she *didn't* see. There wasn't a single plant or a single knick-knack anywhere in sight. No sign of any decorative touches anywhere she looked.

Definitely a bachelor pad. Something like relief went through her. Had she been expecting something different? No. Maybe. Not really.

Okay, maybe she had been a little worried that Adam wasn't really single, which was ridiculous. Of course he was single. Why would someone who looked like him settle down with just one woman when he could have his pick of different women every night of the week?

Stop it.

She didn't need to be thinking like that right now, not when she was standing here in the middle of Adam's living room. Beth wasn't stupid—she knew he saw other women. She'd met him in a chatroom, for crying out loud. To hook-up. For sex. Of course he was seeing other women.

She still didn't need to be thinking about that right now. It didn't matter who else he saw or what else he did—she was the one here with him now.

Although she wasn't entirely sure why, not after what had happened in the parking lot. Heat rushed to her face and she turned around, trying to hide it in case Adam noticed. Oh God, just thinking about what they'd done—what *she'd* done—was enough to send her scurrying in embarrassment.

And enough to cause warmth to grow between her legs and her breath to shorten with excitement. She didn't understand it, all these conflicting emotions and reactions. Yes, she was embarrassed, both by what they'd done and how she had reacted. But she was also extremely turned on—more turned on than she had been in a long time.

Unless you counted the last two times she'd been with Adam.

Tonight had to be the last time she met with him. It would be too easy to fall for him, too easy to view this whole thing—whatever it was—as a relationship. Part of her wondered if maybe she wasn't already in over her head. No, she couldn't be. It was just sex, nothing else.

Or so she thought until today. Spending the day with Adam, getting to know his co-workers and hanging out as if she belonged there—it had been a mistake. A big one. She'd gotten to know Adam today—about him, as a person. His likes and dislikes, the way one eyebrow cocked up in disbelief whenever he disagreed with something one of his co-workers said. The way he was able to laugh at himself if he made a mistake. The way he actually listened to people when they spoke, as if whatever they were saying was important.

It had only been one day but he seemed more real to her now. A real man, with likes and dislikes and quirks, instead of a hot body meant for nothing more than sexual gratification.

Oh, who was she kidding? She liked him—a lot. Had from that very first night together.

So yeah, tonight *had* to be their last time together. It had to be.

"You can take your jacket off, you know. I won't bite. Unless you want me to, of course, then I'll be happy to oblige." Adam came to a stop next to her, a bottle of beer in his outstretched hand. When had he gone to the kitchen?

Beth shrugged out of the jacket then accepted the beer from him. She took a small sip, her eyes darting around the room, unable to meet his gaze. Could he tell what she was thinking? God, she hoped not.

He must have noticed her looking around because he stepped closer, heat from his body washing over her. She turned, his gaze catching hers as he offered her a quick smile that exposed the small dimple in his cheek. "It's not much but it's home. A place to crash and study. And it's clean. Well, mostly."

"It's, uh, nice." She raised the bottle to her mouth and took a small swallow. Could Adam see the flush spreading across her face? Probably. There didn't seem to be much that he missed.

"Do you want the ten-cent tour?"

Was that his way of inviting her back to his room? It must be—she couldn't imagine there being much more to the apartment than what she was seeing from her vantage point.

"Um...okay."

Adam grinned again and grabbed her free hand, tugging her along as he pointed out each room. "The living room, obviously. There's a small balcony outside. This building backs up to the woods so it's nice during the summer." He pointed to the sliding glass doors hidden by heavy drapes then took several steps closer to the darkened hallway. "Kitchen, with all the modern amenities, of course."

"Of course."

He chuckled and pointed to the left. "Formal dining room, such as it is. I usually just eat at the counter." He took the beer from her and placed it on the table along with his, then led her into the hallway, palming a switch as he kept walking. "Laundry closet—yes, I know how to do laundry."

Beth laughed, some of her nervousness fading away. Was he trying to make her feel more at ease? She didn't know and realized it didn't matter. Not right now.

"We have a fully modern bathroom through this door here. Don't look too close, I probably left the toilet seat up. Spare room is through that door there. I like to think of it as an office, but it's more of a catch-all."

"Every house should have one."

"Exactly. A woman after my own heart." He gave her another grin then pushed open the door to his left. He led her inside then reached behind her and palmed another switch. Soft light from a small lamp on the bedside table filled the room.

"And this—" Adam's voice lowered to a husky whisper, one filled with promise. "This is the bedroom."

Beth nodded, unable to speak. Heat spiraled out from her center, spinning faster and faster, leaving her breathless. Her gaze fastened on the dark cherry sleigh bed in the center of the room. A set of wooden steps, two high, led up to the king size monstrosity. A thick comforter in a deep maroon pattern was stretched over matching sheets that glimmered in the dim light. It was…opulent. Enticing. Exciting.

Frightening.

She must have made a small noise, a little sigh or

croak of surprise, because Adam's hand was suddenly in the middle of her back, warm and comforting. He turned her around, his dark blue gaze capturing hers, searching.

There was something about the look in his eyes, something different. Heat and desire were there, yes. Need, even. But no teasing and none of the playfulness that she had noticed their last two times together, or even earlier tonight in the parking light.

The air around them grew heavy, warm. Her breath caught in her throat and her heart slammed against her chest before racing in a crazy rhythm. She almost pulled away, almost ran from the room, from his apartment.

Not from fear. Some inner instinct told her she had nothing to fear from Adam. No, this was something entirely different. A survival instinct, screaming at her to save herself. Warning her of...something.

But she didn't move. She *couldn't* move, not when Adam's deep gaze held her in place. He reached up with one hand and gently cupped her cheek. His thumb swept across her lower lip, the touch light, tentative. Beth's eyes fluttered closed as a small sigh escaped her.

And then his mouth was on hers. Soft, so soft. Tender. Seeking permission. Beth swayed closer, leaning into the kiss, granting him the permission he was silently seeking.

Adam deepened the kiss, his tongue sweeping in and dancing with hers. Slow, gentle. Like she was a treasured chalice of rare nectar that he wanted to savor. Beth sighed and wrapped her arms around his neck, her body melting under the tender onslaught. Gentle hands, large and warm, skimmed along her side, sliding her blouse up as they went. Adam broke the kiss with a low moan and pulled the shirt over her head, tossing it to the side. Flesh—she wanted to feel bare flesh to bare flesh. No, it was much more than want. This was *need*—primal, basic, potent. Powerful, oh so powerful.

She ran her hands over his chest and down his sides, catching the hem of his shirt with her fingers. She slid it up, her palms grazing hot flesh along the way. His heart beat steady against her hand, a fast, heavy pounding that filled her with awe.

With power.

She was the one making his heart beat so fast. *She* was the one making the breath hitch in his chest and causing his eyes to glaze with passion and need.

With desire.

Beth eased the shirt over his head, let it drop to the floor as she pressed a soft kiss in the middle of his chest. Right there, where the small thatch of hair grew before trailing in a thin line to disappear into the waistband of his jeans. She spread her fingers wide against his broad chest, reveled in the feel of him. Hard and soft. Warm, so warm, his skin tanned, darker than the pale flesh of her hands.

Need coursed through her, so different than the need of their previous encounters. She needed to touch, to feel. To learn every inch of the magnificent body before her.

To have memories later, when this was all over? No, she wouldn't think about that now. There was no future. No past. Just…now.

Beth trailed her mouth along his chest, peppering his skin with light kisses. She pressed her mouth against his heart, felt the heavy pounding and heard the sharp hiss of his breath.

Lower, lower still, her mouth following that thin line of darker blonde hair. Her hands closed over the button of his jeans, her trembling fingers struggling to undo it. Adam's hands closed over hers, strong and rough. Large hands, dark against hers, rough and calloused yet oh so gentle.

He helped her undo the button, gently guided her hands as she slid the zipper down. Her fingers dipped into the waistband of his jeans, tugged them past his waist until the heavy length of his erection popped free.

She closed her hand around him, marveling at the softness of skin stretched tight. Thick, powerful. She slid her hand along the hardened length as she kissed her way down his chest, his stomach, down lower to the paler skin of hips and groin.

Adam slid his hands into her hair, threading his fingers through the long strands. But instead of guiding her to his erection, instead of holding her in place, he gently tugged and pulled her up. Something flared in his eyes, something that made her heart stammer in her chest. Then his mouth was on hers, the kiss almost desperate somehow.

He picked her up, his mouth still on hers, and carried her over to the bed. Beth's hands dug into his shoulders, certain he would drop her, afraid she was too heavy for him, worried he would somehow hurt himself by lifting her.

The worry was misplaced. He climbed the steps and gently lowered her to the mattress, shifting her to the side as he pulled the comforter back. The smooth coolness of silky sheets touched her back, thrilling and decadent. Adam climbed onto the mattress and knelt beside her, his eyes dark pools of desire as he slid the skirt down her legs.

There was something about the way he looked at her, something about the blatant need in his eyes that frightened her. This was different, so different from their other encounters.

No. No, she was just reading into it. There was nothing between them, just casual sex. That was all. To read anything else into it was foolish. Dangerous.

His mouth closed over hers once more, the kiss deeper this time. His hands roamed over her body, touching her everywhere except where she needed to be touched. Her hands closed over his shoulders, her body arching, trying to reach for the touch she needed so badly.

Adam broke the kiss and stared down at her. Intense. Searching...but for what?

"You're the first woman I've had here in over eight months." His voice was a husky whisper, rough yet intimate. Beth struggled to understand the words, struggled to understand why he uttered them.

Struggled to convince herself they didn't mean anything, cautioned herself not to read into them.

Then Adam's mouth was on hers again, gentle but demanding as he slid the jeans down his powerful legs and kicked them off. He shifted on top of her, sheathing himself with a condom he'd pulled out when she wasn't looking. His body, so big and powerful, stretched along her own. Beth wrapped her legs around his waist, her hips thrusting up. Reaching. Searching.

Adam's hands closed over hers, stretched them above her head and held them in place. He broke the kiss, his gaze capturing hers with a frightening intensity as he entered her in one swift move.

Beth's head fell back, her lids fluttering closed as sensation washed over her. More, she needed more—

"Look at me, Beth. Look at me."

No. She couldn't. She was afraid to.

But she was helpless to ignore the commanding plea in his voice. She struggled to force her eyes open, struggled against herself to meet his gaze.

And plunged over the edge into a waterfall of shimmering lights that exploded around her.

Chapter Twelve

"Beth seems like a nice girl."

Adam looked up from the study guide, surprised to see Dale leaning in the doorway. Where the hell had he come from? Yeah, Adam had been focused on studying but he still should have heard the other man approaching through the bunk room.

"Yeah, I guess."

"You guess? Seriously?"

"Okay. She *is* nice. Does that make you feel better?"

"It's not me who needs to feel better."

Adam frowned, considered asking Dale what the hell he was talking about, then changed his mind. He didn't feel like having a conversation about Beth. Hell, he didn't feel like having a conversation about *anything*. He'd been in a foul mood for the last seven days, ever since dropping Beth off at her car the morning after he made the mistake of taking her back to her place.

Mistake. Yeah, right. It had been more than a mistake. What the fuck had he been thinking? He never took women back to his place. *Never*. So why the hell had he broken his own rules with Beth?

He'd been asking himself that question for the last week and the only answer he could come up with pissed him off.

Guilt.

Pure, unmitigated guilt.

What he didn't understand is *why*. Guilt over what? The only thing between them was sex. Nothing more, nothing less. This was no different than any other hook-up he'd had in the last eight months. Hook-up, fuck a few times, go their separate ways. That was the way it was supposed to work. No complications, no guilt.

Except it wasn't going that way with Beth, and it fucking pissed him off. She wasn't supposed to be any different than the other women he'd fucked.

Except she was.

And what they'd done a week ago in his bed wasn't *fucking*. It had been…different. It was like he couldn't get enough of her and he didn't know why.

She was different, and that worried him. Was it because this was all new to her? Could it be as simple as some kind of warped, misplaced protectiveness he felt for her? But *why?*

That's what it all came down to—the why. But damn if he had the fucking answer to it.

They'd had their three times together. By his own rules, it was done and over with. He hadn't called her. Hadn't sent her a text. Fair enough, since she hadn't called or texted him, either. And he hadn't checked in the chatroom to see if she was in there.

He hadn't been in the chatroom at all. Every single time he thought about logging on, his stomach clenched and filled with bile—because he was afraid he'd see Beth there, looking for a hook-up. The idea of her being with anyone else—

He couldn't even finish the thought, not without running the risk of having his dinner come right back up.

"Are you okay?"

"What?" Adam raised his head and scowled at Dale. "Fine. Why?"

"Because you haven't heard a single word I said. And you look like you're ready to hurl."

"I'm fine. Just studying, that's all."

"If you say so." Dale shifted, ran one hand through his brown hair, then crossed his arms in front of his chest. "So, are you and Beth a thing now?"

"Fuck no. You should know better."

"Really?"

"Yeah, really. I don't date. I don't have relationships. You know that."

"Then why the hell did you bring her with you last week? Sure looked like a date to me."

"It wasn't a date. I just didn't feel like listening to everyone give me shit if I showed up solo."

"Not sure if I'm buying that."

"I don't give a shit what you're buying. It was just a hook-up, that's all. Nothing more to it than that."

Dale studied him through a frown. A minute went by, then another, until Adam started to squirm in the ancient desk chair. *Squeak. Squeak. Squeak.* Rusty springs creaked with each movement and he had to force himself to stay still.

But Dale kept looking at him, his gaze penetrating and completely unreadable. Adam finally slammed the book closed. "Why the fuck are you staring at me like that?"

"Just trying to figure out if I should tell you or not."

"Tell me *what?*"

Dale shrugged then pushed away from the doorframe. "Nothing. It's not important."

"Bullshit. You can't say something like that then just turn around and walk away. Now out with it. Tell me what?"

"Nothing. It doesn't matter, not really."

"You have got to be kidding me. Stop the fucking games already."

"No games. I was just going to give you some advice, that's all."

"Yeah? This ought to be good. What kind of advice could you possibly give me?"

"Just that the next time you feel like playing around in a parking lot, you should make sure the fucking interior light is turned off."

Dale's words slammed into him, robbing him of breath for a painfully long second. Heat rushed to Adam's face and he looked away, feeling like he'd just been caught with his hand in the cookie jar.

Hell, he *had* been caught.

He ran both hands over his face then up through his hair. "Fuck. Seriously? How much did you see?"

"Enough to know what the fuck you were doing."

"Shit. Why the hell are you just now telling me this? Why didn't you say something our first day in?"

"Because I wasn't sure you really needed to know. I'm still not sure."

"Fuck. Did anyone else see?" Not that it was a big deal, not really. So what if they'd been seen? Beth had been covered—from the waist up, anyway. No way would anyone have been able to see lower than her chest, not while she was sitting in the passenger seat. And he'd been covered too, hidden by the open door of his SUV. It wasn't like anyone could have actually seen him jerking off or shooting his wad over the gravel lot.

And so what if they had? Big deal. He'd done a hell of a lot more, things that would raise everyone's eyebrows if they learned about them. Being caught jerking off was pretty fucking mild.

But it wasn't the idea of anyone seeing him—he didn't care about that. Beth was a different story. The idea that someone had witnessed Beth being fingerfucked, that someone else had seen her reaction and watched how she came undone when she climaxed…that was enough to send his blood boiling. Nobody else had a right to witness that. Nobody else had a right to see the intensity—the honesty—of her reactions.

Adam pushed out of the chair, too nervous to sit. He spun around in a circle, jammed his clenched fists into the front pockets of his pants, and glared at Dale. "Well? Who else saw?"

"Nobody. Just me and Melanie. She didn't realize what was going on at first. She wanted to go over and say goodnight. I had to stop her and explain."

"Great. Just fucking great. Wonderful." Adam didn't know whether to laugh—or punch a wall. It was too easy to imagine Melanie's bright smile as she walked over, totally oblivious to what was going on until it was too late.

"That's it, nobody else?"

"Not that I know of, no."

"Yeah, well." Adam shifted, cleared his throat. "I'll

keep that in mind next time. Sorry you had to explain."

"I didn't tell you for you to apologize. I told you because I don't know if you know what the fuck you're doing."

"What the hell is that supposed to mean?"

"Look, Beth seemed like a nice girl. You should probably stop and think before you use someone like that—"

"I wasn't using her so you can just stop that bullshit now."

"No? You sure about that? Listen, I know you're into some weird shit. Whatever. To each his own. Whatever makes you happy. But I get the feeling Beth isn't like that—"

"How the hell do you think I met her? Trust me, it was a mutually beneficial arrangement. Nobody was using anybody."

Surprise flared in Dale's eyes and he quickly looked away. He blew out a quick breath then turned back to Adam. "So she really wasn't a date, then? There's really nothing going on between you two?"

"No, she wasn't, and no, there isn't."

"Sorry. My mistake, then. I shouldn't have brought it up."

"Yeah, whatever. No big deal."

Dale nodded then turned around to leave. He'd gone two steps before stopping and turning back. "By the way, Melanie says you're both the same shade of green."

Adam rolled his eyes. Dale's girlfriend was an artist who swore she saw people and things in terms of colors. Not auras, but real, honest-to-goodness colors. Whatever the fuck that meant. Melanie was a sweet woman, always friendly and open, but sometimes the weirdest shit came out of her mouth. Adam had learned months ago not to question it, to just nod and change the conversation to something not quite so woo-woo.

And he didn't want to ask, knew he shouldn't. But he couldn't stop himself. "Okay. We're green. What the hell does that even mean?"

"No fucking clue. But she said it was odd that two people had almost the exact same color. Same, but different."

"You know you're starting to sound as out there as she does, right?"

"Hey, I'm just telling you what she said. She also said yours was growing darker, the edges turning black. That worried her for some reason."

Adam rolled his eyes again. "Yeah, okay. Thanks for the warning."

Dale chuckled then turned to leave. He stopped again with a grunt of impatience. "Before I forget. Lauren said Kenny's getting us tickets to the hockey game next week. You in?"

Lauren, Dale's sister, was engaged to Kenny Haskell, a professional hockey player for the Baltimore Banners. Adam wasn't sure why, but Kenny would occasionally get a bunch of tickets for them—and they were usually great seats in the lower bowl. Adam tried to go whenever he had the chance.

"Yeah, I'm in. I could go for some hockey."

"One or two?"

"One or two what?"

"Tickets. Do you want one or two?"

Adam opened his mouth, ready to tell him he only needed one. He changed his mind at the last minute. "Two."

Dale's brows shot up in surprise but he didn't say anything, just nodded and turned to leave once more. Adam held his breath, waiting for him to turn back a third time, but he didn't.

He released the breath he'd been holding then moved back to the desk and lowered himself into the chair. He opened the book he'd been studying but couldn't focus on the words. His concentration was shot. Hell, it had been shot even before Dale came in and bothered him.

It had been shot for the last seven days, ever since he dropped Beth off at her car. He couldn't stop thinking about her, couldn't stop the irrational guilt he felt whenever an image of her popped into his mind.

He needed to do something to get over this…whatever the hell this was. Not another hook-up—he wasn't in the mood, figured he probably just needed a break. So maybe a date. A real date. Surely he could find someone to ask out. He had the perfect excuse now: the hockey game.

That's exactly what he'd do. Find a date to take to the game. He had a week to find someone. Not a problem.

No problem at all.

Chapter Thirteen

Beth squeezed a small amount of styling gel into her palm, rubbed her hands together, then ran them through the woman's hair. A little lift, some smoothing and shaping, and she was done.

Beth stepped back and met the woman's gaze in the mirror. "What do you think?"

The woman was silent for so long that Beth started to worry she didn't like the new style. It was a drastic difference from how she looked when she first came in, with her lifeless silvery-blonde hair pulled back and held in place with an old hair clip. The woman—her name was Linda and she had just turned fifty-six the day after the divorce from her husband of twenty-three years was finalized—had asked for something different. Shorter. Livelier. Younger.

They'd gone over different styles and settled on a short bob with some color added to blend the silver and blonde. Linda had been excited about it when they started just over two hours ago.

Beth held her breath, wondering if the woman was

just as excited now that she was finished.

"It's..." Linda paused, tilting her head from side to side as she studied her reflection in the mirror. Moisture welled in her eyes and she quickly blinked it away. "It's perfect. Perfect."

Beth released a quick sigh and offered the woman a gentle smile. "It is. You look like you're ready to take on the world now."

"I think I really am. Thank you. So much. This is just wonderful." Her smile grew wider as she shook her head, the stylish cut swaying with the movement. Beth removed the cape then spun the chair around so the woman could stand. She followed her to the register and rang her up, surprised at the fifty-dollar tip the woman gave her.

"Thank you so much. This is just the change I so desperately needed."

"I'm glad you like it. Change is good, right?"

The woman paused, her head tilted to the side, a thoughtful frown on her face. "I didn't think so. Not at first. But now...I think you're right. Change *is* a good thing."

Beth stiffened in surprise when the woman gave her a big hug before walking out. She glanced around the empty waiting area, quickly straightened the magazines and style books, then went back to her station to clean up. The salon was closing soon and the only people left were her and Courtney.

"Another happy customer. Good for you." Courtney sat down in her chair and gently spun it from side-to-side, a haunted smile on her face. Something was bothering her best friend, but she didn't know what. And Courtney refused to tell her, no matter how many times she asked. Beth was fairly certain it had something to do with her son, Noah.

And maybe even a man.

Beth tossed the hair clippings into the trash, wiped down her station, then sat down across from Courtney. "You heard what she said about change, didn't you?"

"Yeah. Why?"

"Oh, no reason. Just, you know, trying to figure out what's been going on with you. That's all."

Courtney's gaze became guarded and she looked away. "Nothing is going on with me."

"Really? Because you've been pretty distracted the last couple of weeks."

"I'm fine."

"Is everything okay with Noah?"

"He's fine, too."

"Your mom?"

"Couldn't be better."

"That guy you're seeing?"

Courtney's head spun around, her eyes narrowing as she met Beth's gaze. "There is no guy."

"You know I'm going to figure it out eventually, right? You might as well just tell me now and save me the stress of guessing."

"How's your fireman doing?"

"Changing the subject isn't going to work. And he's doing fine." At least, as far as Beth knew, Adam was doing fine. They hadn't talked in almost two weeks, not since that morning when he dropped her off at his car. And then she received a text from him the night before last, asking if she wanted to go to a hockey game. His shift was going and he had an extra ticket, did she want to join him?

And like a fool, Beth had said yes. They arranged to meet at the Park-and-Ride off I-83 in Hereford tomorrow evening and that had been that. No calls, no more texts. Nothing but silence.

Beth refused to think about it—thinking about it only led to confusion and a headache. She kept telling herself that there was nothing between them. That what they were doing was only sex. That was it, nothing more.

Only that last night together—when Adam had taken her back to his apartment—had felt like it was more than just sex. She thought they had been making love, had hoped that maybe Adam felt the same way. And how stupid was that? Not stupid—dangerous. They'd met in a chatroom for a hook-up. Beth knew Adam wasn't a newcomer there, knew he was probably hooking up with different women every week. Maybe even every night. It was dangerous to think there could be anything between them.

Courtney leaned forward, a glimmer of excitement dancing in her eyes. "So tell me more about him. Is this like a real thing between you two?"

"Good God, no. I don't want a *thing*." She almost choked on the lie, reached for her bottle of water and took a long swallow to cover it up. "We're just having fun. That's all I can handle right now, especially after all the shit I went through when I was with Ed. You know that."

"Ed was a bastard. I tried telling you that from the beginning. I never did like him. And the way he treated you, always knocking you—"

"I know. Trust me, I know. But that's all in the past. Right now, I just want to have a little fun." Beth spun her chair around and studied her reflection in the mirror. Was it obvious she was lying? Could Courtney tell?

But she *wasn't* lying. She really wasn't. She *did* want to have fun. Nothing else. She didn't want a relationship, not right now. Not after suffering so much humiliation before. Being with Ed had caused so many self-esteem issues for her, issues she was still getting over.

Those few times with Adam had helped. He made her feel…special. Beautiful. Wanted. The way he treated her, like her curves were beautiful instead of bulging fat to be ashamed of. The way he made her feel when they were together—

She needed to stop that line of thinking. Right now. Yes, he treated her well. But she was sure he treated all his partners that way. It meant nothing. And she didn't need a man to define her self-worth—that was a lesson she'd had to learn the hard way.

But that didn't mean she didn't need a man for sex. And sex with Adam was…delicious. Until he'd taken her back to his place. Until he'd told her she was the first woman he'd had there in over eight months.

Stop it. Just stop.

Beth forced a smile to her face and turned back to Courtney. "We're supposed to go out tomorrow night. To a hockey game."

Surprise flared in Courtney's eyes. "A hockey game?"

"Yeah. Down in Baltimore."

Courtney's shoulders sagged in relief. Beth frowned, watching her, wondering what she had just missed. "Why do you look so—I don't know. Surprised? Anxious? What are you not telling me?"

"Nothing. Why would you think that?"

"Because of that look in your eyes when I said we were going to a hockey game."

"You're just imagining things."

Beth narrowed her eyes, wondering if she should push the issue. Courtney was lying. Hiding something. Would she tell her if she pushed a little more?

Probably not.

She turned back to the mirror and studied her reflection for a few silent minutes. She ran one hand through her hair, pulling the wavy ends out and holding them in front of her eyes. "You know, I think it's time for a change, too."

"What are you talking about?"

"My hair. I need a change." Beth dropped her hand and turned back to Courtney. "Are you in a hurry to get home?"

"Why?"

"I was just wondering if you felt like doing my hair, that's all."

Courtney glanced at her watch. "I can probably stay. Let me call home and tell my mom I'm going to be running late."

"Is that going to be a problem? I don't want—"

"Nope, no problem at all. You know me—no life."

"Great. You call home, and I'll get everything together." Beth pushed out of the chair and walked to the back room. She studied the different tubes of color, mixing them in her mind, imagining how each would look on her. Excitement coursed through her when she made a final decision.

Change. Yes. This was exactly what she needed. A drastic change. Something totally different.

She mixed everything together, gathered the needed supplies, then placed everything on a small rolling cart and wheeled it out. Courtney studied the bowls and tubes of color.

"Are you sure? That's pretty different."

"Positive." Beth draped a cape around her shoulders then took a seat at Courtney's station. She leaned forward, grabbed a pair of scissors, and passed them over her shoulder. "But first, I want you to cut off a good five inches."

"Five inches? Beth, are you sure? I thought you liked your hair long."

"This is all in the name of change."

Courtney's gaze met hers in the mirror. Several long seconds went by before she reached out and took the scissors from Beth's hand. "I hope you know what you're doing."

"Not a clue."

"It's going to be too late to change your mind once I cut—"

"I know. Just do it."

"Are you sure?"

"Yes."

"Positively sure?"

"Yes—absolutely, positively, one hundred percent certain."

Courtney frowned, the disbelief clear on her face. She gathered the ends of Beth's hair and held the thick hank in one hand and the scissors in the other. "You're sure you're sure?"

"Just do it already!"

Courtney nodded, took a deep breath—and cut. Beth gasped, which made Courtney freeze, a horrified expression on her face. "You told me to do it!"

Beth laughed, the sound clear and somehow cleansing. She wiped her eyes and looked at Courtney. "I was only teasing you. I need this. Now get to it.

Change awaits."

"I think you need your head examined."

Beth's smile faded, just a little. No, it wasn't her head she needed examined.

It was her heart.

But she wasn't about to tell Courtney that. She could barely admit it to herself. Hadn't she learned her lesson already? How could she have let herself start falling for Adam?

Sex. Just sex. She had to keep telling herself that. Tomorrow night would be their last time together. It had to be. She couldn't risk anything happening. Couldn't risk falling even harder for him.

One last time and that would be it. She was turning over a brand-new leaf. Moving on.

Changing.

She hoped.

Chapter Fourteen

The noise level was deafening, screams and shouts echoing from the high ceiling, bouncing off the ice. Adam was on his feet, clapping and cheering with everyone else after the Banners evened the score—again. The game had gone back and forth all through the first period, ending with Columbus up by one. That changed in the second period…and kept changing as each team shot the puck into the net. The crowd was energized, the excitement so thick he could almost taste it.

The downside was that the noise made conversation almost impossible, unless you felt like shouting. Adam wasn't a shouter, which meant he was saved from trying to talk.

Which was a good thing, because he didn't feel like answering questions. He had to be blind to miss the looks he received when he walked in with Beth—looks he was still getting. Curious. Questioning. Thoughtful. Even one that was less than complimentary from Dale.

Did Beth notice them? Christ, he hoped not. How

the hell would he even begin to explain them if she did and asked what they were for? It wasn't like he could tell her the reasons for them.

Not like he could admit that he'd pretty much told everyone that she was nothing more than a casual date that first night and that they'd never see her again.

Dale had pulled him aside earlier and actually came close to cussing him out. Accused him of using Beth. Told him he needed his fucking head examined. Adam hadn't bothered to reply, just turned and walked away.

What the fuck did Dale know? Nothing. Absolutely nothing. And it wasn't like Adam had planned on bringing Beth when he said he needed a second ticket. He hadn't, not even close.

But he hadn't figured it would be so hard to find anyone else to bring. Where the hell did normal people go to meet dates, anyway? Adam didn't date, had never needed to go out and try to meet women. If he wanted some action, he simply logged onto his computer or phone and set something up and that was it. Quick, easy. Painless.

He couldn't do that for a date, though. Not a real date, one that involved actually going somewhere in public. After banging his head against the wall in frustration, he finally broke down and sent Beth a text, asking her if she wanted to go.

A fucking text. Because calling her had been out of the question. Calling her would have made it seem too much like an actual date.

No way in hell was Adam going there, even if he *had* expected her to say no. Part of him was still surprised she said yes.

He glanced at her from the corner of his eye,

trying to watch her without being obvious about it. It still took a few seconds for his mind to register that she was the same person he had met close to three months ago. Had it been that long already? It didn't feel like it.

And she really did look different. The new hairstyle completely changed her appearance. The long thick waves of dark hair were gone, replaced by a loosely-swinging asymmetrical cut that draped her shoulders. The dark hair was lighter now, more of a deep blonde with bold streaks of copper that ended in tips that were almost white.

But it wasn't just the hair that was different. She seemed...lighter, somehow. More confident. A little bolder.

So what the hell had happened to change her? And why the hell had he experienced an insane flash of jealousy when a few of the guys lavished compliments on her? He'd had an unexplainable urge to ram his fist into Jay's face earlier—which made no sense considering how head-over-heels in love Jay was with Angie.

Beth leaned to the side, listening to whatever Angie was saying, then tossed her head back and laughed. Jay said something as well, which only made Beth laugh harder.

What the hell was up with that?

Adam shifted in the hard seat and tried to pretend he didn't feel like an outsider. Fuck. Beth was *his* date. Why the hell should he feel like an outsider?

Enough of that bullshit.

He draped his arm around Beth's shoulders and pulled her closer, leaning down so his mouth was close to her ear. "Having fun?"

Beth gave him an odd look then nodded before

easing away from him and turning to say something to Angie.

What the fuck?

Adam dropped his arm and reached for the large plastic cup of beer. Did she just blow him off? Really?

The horn sounded again, long and loud. Everyone around him jumped to their feet, including Beth. Her elbow bumped his arm; beer sloshed over the rim of the cup and splashed across his shirt and jeans.

"OhmyGod. I'm so sorry."

Adam looked up, saw the look of genuine horror on Beth's face as she grabbed a napkin and tried to sop up the mess. The paper napkin disintegrated, leaving a trail of white shreds wherever it touched.

Adam reached for her hand and removed the napkin before she could do any more damage. "It's fine. Really. My fault."

"I should have watched—"

"Really. It's not a big deal. I'll just go—"

"I'll get more napkins." Beth was already threading her way down the aisle before Adam could say anything. He stared after her for a confused second then shook his head and pulled the wet shirt away from his stomach.

The horn sounded again and everyone around him started standing. Adam looked around, wondering if he had missed another goal, then realized it was nothing more than the end of the second period.

He muttered to himself, wondering if he could use being drenched in beer as an excuse to leave early. He'd had that thought earlier, thinking maybe he could convince Beth to go somewhere else—somewhere a lot more private. Now, after the way she had just acted, he wasn't so sure.

Adam didn't like the feeling.

No, he was probably reading too much into things. Beth wouldn't have joined him tonight if she wasn't looking forward to the alone time later. Right?

Maybe.

Then again, maybe not.

And Christ, if this was what dating felt like, he wanted no parts of it. Give him the sure thing any day and he'd be happy.

"Way to impress your date, asshole."

Adam looked over, saw Dale scowling at him. Not just Dale—Jay as well. "What the hell is that supposed to mean?"

"You've been sitting there all night acting like you'd rather be anywhere else."

"What are you talking about? I haven't—"

"Yeah, you have." Jay moved into Beth's empty seat the same time Dale moved to stand in front of him. Great, they were ganging up on him. Just what he didn't need right now.

"If you didn't want to be around Beth, why the hell did you even bring her?"

"What makes you think I don't want to be around her?"

"The way you're sitting there, with all that attitude, looking like you'd rather be anywhere else but here."

Adam frowned. What the hell was Jay talking about? He hadn't been acting like that, not at all. "Beth is the one acting like she doesn't want to be here, not me."

"Probably because she can sense it."

"Oh, bullshit. There's nothing to sense, so I'm not buying it."

Dale folded his arms across his chest, a frown on

his face as he studied Adam. "Why'd you bring her, anyway? I thought you said there wasn't anything between you two."

"There's not."

"Then why bring her?"

Anger went through him, sharp and brittle. "What the hell do you care? Seriously, it's none of your damned business."

Dale stepped back, his hands held up in mock surrender. "Whoa. Excuse the piss out of me."

Fuck. What the hell was his problem? What had caused that flash of anger and the unusual outburst?

He ran one hand over his face and blew out a deep breath. "Sorry. I didn't mean to yell. I don't know what the hell got into me."

Jay leaned closed, shoved Adam in the shoulder, then stole his beer. "Well whatever it is, you need to get over it if you want to see Beth again."

"It's not like that. We're not dating."

"Really? This is the second time you've brought her to a shift outing. What the hell do you call it?"

"Nothing. We're just hanging out. I don't date. You know that. And you know why, too." Jay, of all people, should understand exactly why. He had walked in on his wife years ago and caught her with someone else. The divorce had been quick and brutal—apparently as quick and brutal as the marriage—and ended with Jay swearing off relationships. Yeah, he was with Angie now, but it had taken him years to get to that point.

And maybe Jay hadn't been hooking up like Adam did, but he hadn't exactly been a monk, either. If anyone could understand Adam's position, it had to be Jay.

Only he wasn't looking at Adam with understanding. He saw more pity than anything else in the other man's gray eyes—pity he didn't want *or* need.

"Yeah, I do know why. Take it from experience—you can't let getting fucked over in the past rule your whole life."

"I'm not."

"Then stop acting like an asshole. Don't lead this girl on."

"I'm not *leading her on*. It's a mutual thing. You wouldn't understand."

"Mutual, huh?"

"Yeah. *Mutual*. We're just having fun. That's it. I probably won't even see her after—"

Dale kicked him in the shin, hard. Adam jerked his leg back, ready to read the other man the riot act. Dale simply shook his head and pointed at something over Adam's shoulder. Adam turned, his heart dropping to a point somewhere below his stomach. Angie, Melanie, and Beth were walking down the aisle behind them.

Fuck. Had Beth heard? Had any of them? No, they couldn't have. They were too far away to hear, especially with all the other noise. No way did they hear.

Adam shot a desperate glance in Jay's direction. The other man shared a quick look with Dale then shook his head. "I think you're good. For now."

Relief flooded through Adam but it was short-lived, replaced by guilt. What the hell would he have done if Beth had overheard him? How the fuck would he have explained that?

Things had gone too far. He should have never brought her tonight. He should have never taken her back to his place the other week.

And he sure as hell should have never told her she was the only woman he'd had in his own bed in the last eight months.

She stopped and leaned down, a thick stack of napkins in one hand and a fresh beer in the other. A small smile teased the corners of her mouth as she handed him the pile of napkins. "It'll probably be less messy if you do it."

"Yeah. No problem." Adam grabbed the napkins and absently wiped at his shirt and jeans, quickly mopping up most of the damage. It didn't matter, it was just beer. Not like it wouldn't wash out, anyway. As long as he didn't get pulled over on his way home and have to explain why he smelled like a brewery, it would be fine. Hell, everything would probably be dried by then anyway.

He placed the used napkins in the cup holder to his left then glanced up at the large screen suspended above the ice. Only a few minutes left in the intermission. He shifted in the seat, wondering why Beth was still standing behind him, ready to ask her just that. She leaned down, that small smile still on her face, and whispered in his ear.

"Would you mind if we left early?"

Adam froze, guilt and confusion swirling inside him. Had she heard him earlier? Is that why she wanted to leave? He studied her face, searching for anger or hurt or disappointment. The only thing he saw was a hint of barely concealed desire and excitement.

He hesitated, blinked a few times, wondering if he was seeing things that weren't there. Why the sudden change, after she seemed so...so aloof earlier? Or maybe he had been reading into *that* instead. It didn't matter, not when his body was already reacting to the heat of her breath against his skin, to the desire in her eyes.

"Uh, no. No, that's fine."

She rewarded him with a sultry smile that heated the blood pounding through his veins. Adam cleared his throat and pushed out of the seat, nearly knocking over two cups of beer. He muttered something to Dale and Jay, ignoring their pointed looks as he brushed past them. He stopped long enough to kick Jay in the ankle when the man called him an ass, then kept going, meeting Beth at the end of the aisle. He grabbed her hand and hurried up the concrete stairs, fighting against the swarm of people coming down to take their seats.

His heart was racing with anticipation by the time they reached the parking garage. The sound of their footsteps against the cracked concrete floor echoed around them, oddly loud in the surrounding emptiness. Adam pressed a button on his key fob, heard two short beeps from the horn of his SUV as it unlocked.

He stopped in front of the passenger door, pulled it open for Beth. She was about to climb in when he pulled her into his arms and caught her mouth with his. The kiss was deep, hungry, filled with a need that made his stomach clench in anticipation. Hot, potent, primal.

Beth sighed, a throaty little moan that sent even more blood surging to his cock. She leaned against him, her hands digging into his shoulders as he deepened the kiss. And fuck, he needed to stop. Now. If he didn't, he'd turn her around, shove those curve-hugging jeans down past her ass, bend her over, and fuck her right here.

The image of her bent over in front of him seared his mind. Fuck, yes. He could see it now, imagined the way her tight pussy would clench his cock as he pounded into her from behind. Deep, so fucking deep. Filling her—

Adam pulled away with a groan, afraid he'd do exactly that. Right here. Right now. He couldn't. Hadn't their last time in a parking lot taught him anything? He blew out a sigh and looked up, saw the small security cameras attached to the ceiling above them.

Yeah, not going to happen. Not here. Not now.

He took another step back and offered Beth a crooked smile. "How about we continue this somewhere else? There's too much of an audience right now."

"Audience?" Her voice was low, just above a whisper, a little dazed. He nodded and motioned toward the cameras overhead. Her gaze followed, her eyes widening in surprise when she noticed them. A flush spread across her cheeks and she took a hurried step back, looking everywhere but at him.

Adam bit back a chuckle and helped her into the SUV. "So. Where to now? We, uh, we could go back to my place and—"

But Beth was shaking her head already, interrupting him. "I have to work in the morning. That's why I asked if we could leave early. Could you just take me back to my car?"

Adam blinked, quickly schooled his face to hide his disappointment. Was she telling the truth? Had she heard what he'd said to Jay and Dale? Was that why she wanted to leave? Or was she merely trying to get rid of him?

No, this was Beth. Maybe he didn't know her that well, but he didn't think she would lie. At least, that's what he tried to tell himself.

He finally nodded and gave her a small smile. "Yeah, sure. No problem." He made sure she was belted in before he closed the door then hurried around to the driver side and climbed in.

And tried to convince himself that her rejection meant nothing.

Nothing at all.

Chapter Fifteen

Adam pulled his SUV into the parking lot then backed into the empty slot next to Beth's car. With as quiet as she had been during the long drive back, he half-expected her to jump out and make a run for it. Instead, she shifted sideways in the seat and gave him a small smile.

"I had fun tonight. Thank you."

Fun? Really? He wanted to tell her he didn't quite believe her but what difference did it make? It took too much effort to smile back so he settled for a quick grin, one that would hide his thoughts. "I'm glad. Me, too."

Beth nodded, looked away. But she didn't move, didn't reach for the door handle, didn't lean down to grab her bag off the floor. She twisted her hands in her lap, then reached up and tucked a strand of hair behind her ear. She sighed then shifted in the seat once more, shooting him a quick glance he didn't quite understand.

"Everything okay?"

"Hm? Yes. Fine." She nodded again then ducked her head, pulled her lower lip between her teeth. Adam looked away and swallowed a groan, cursing his body's reaction to just that small sight. His body could react all it wanted—that didn't mean it was going to receive any satisfaction. Not tonight, not here.

Not until he got home, where he could jerk off in private. Alone. Maybe not even then, not unless he could get the image of Beth out of his mind.

So why the hell was she still sitting there? Was she waiting for him to say something? *Should* he say something? Fuck if he knew what, though. His mind was a total blank, still trying to figure out what had happened.

Not just tonight. Two weeks ago, their last night together. Which should have been their last night, period. He should have never asked her to go tonight. He should have just put her from his mind and moved on. That's what he usually did.

That's what he needed to do. Tonight. Now.

But he couldn't just let her leave, not without a kiss goodbye. Just a quick one. A kiss, nothing more.

He undid his seatbelt then leaned across the console, closing the distance separating them. Beth met him halfway, her mouth closing on his before he realized what she was doing.

The kiss was anything but sweet. He tasted her passion, her need. Felt it in the way her trembling fingers caressed his cheek, in the small sigh that moved from her mouth to his. Adam clenched his hand along the edge of the console, forcing himself not to move. To not take control. To let Beth kiss him and leave.

Only she wasn't leaving. This wasn't a kiss to say goodbye, this was a kiss filled with promise. With dark delights and decadent reward. Adam groaned, his body flaring to life, his cock straining against the denim of his jeans.

Fuck. He needed to stop, need to—

Beth slid closer, her hand resting on his thigh as she pushed herself across the console, reaching for him. Adam broke the kiss with a hungry growl, reached down for the lever of his seat and slid it all the way back then hit the recline button. He turned the engine off, killed the headlights, then reached for Beth, pulling her across the console until she was partially draped across his lap.

Then he was kissing her again, his mouth feeding off hers, need and desire exploding within him. He shifted, tried to reach for the hem of her shirt, banged his knee against the steering wheel.

"Fuck." He muttered the word and eased Beth away from him. "Back seat."

Beth nodded, a small smile teasing her mouth, and climbed between the two seats to reach the back. Adam quickly followed her, banging his head against the dome light and his knee against the edge of a cup holder. Beth laughed, the sound low and breathless. Adam answered her smile with one of his own, knowing how ridiculous he must look trying to wedge himself between the two seats.

Then it didn't matter because he was finally next to her, sprawled along the back seat, his arms around her as he claimed her mouth once more. Hot. Hungry. Urgent.

He skimmed his hands along her sides, his fingers curling around the hem of her sweater. Beth grabbed his hands and nudged them away, holding them to the side.

"No. Not yet."

"But—"

"Not yet." A teasing smile curled her lips, heat dancing in her eyes. Then she reached between them and undid the button of his jeans, slid the zipper down. Adam swallowed back a groan and lifted his hips, tried to help her ease the jeans down only to have her shake her head and tell him no.

Her hand curled around his hard length, her touch cool yet searing, burning. One long stroke, then another. He swallowed back a groan, trying to hide his disappointment when she released her hold on him.

"Scoot back so you're against the door."

Adam hesitated but only for a second. He untangled his feet from hers then slid toward the door, settling himself so one leg was stretched out along the seat and the other was hanging over the edge, his foot planted firmly on the floor. Not the most comfortable position but he was sure he'd survive.

Beth kneeled by his stretched-out leg, her head tilted to the side as she studied him. "Reach above you. Grab that handhold with both hands."

Adam looked behind him, reached up and wrapped his hands around the leather-covered handle. "Like this?"

"Yes. Just like that. Don't let go."

Adam grinned. He had no idea what she had planned and he didn't care. Whatever it was, he was certain he was going to enjoy it—but not as much as he enjoyed the confident command in Beth's voice. She'd never taken the lead the other times they were together. This was something new, and not just between them. Adam sensed that being in charge was completely new for her.

And he was more than happy to oblige.

Her hungry gaze traveled along his body, sparking

flames of heat everywhere she looked. His skin prickled beneath his clothes and a bead of sweat broke out along his forehead. Fuck, what was wrong with him? He shouldn't be reacting like this. Except for the jeans shoved down past his hips, he was still fully dressed. She wasn't even fucking touch him.

But he wanted her to. Fuck, he wanted her to touch him so bad he could taste it.

Her gaze drifted to his cock, the thick length standing straight and proud. Eager. Beth's tongue darted out, swiped across her lower lip. She brought one hand to her throat, slid it down across her body, over the fullness of her breasts. Down lower, to the waistband of her jeans, lower still until she tilted her hips against her palm and sighed.

Adam's cock jumped and a small moan escaped him. Beth's hand dropped away, her gaze darting to his. He saw hesitation and uncertainty there and he cursed himself for making a sound.

"Don't stop."

She chewed on her lower lip, the uncertainty slowly fading from her eyes. Adam took another deep breath, let it out slow, held her gaze with his.

"You are so fucking hot, Beth. Let me watch. Show me how you play with that sweet fucking pussy."

Her breath rushed from her in a sharp gasp. Had he gone too far? Had he embarrassed her? He opened his mouth to apologize, to say something reassuring, then snapped it closed when she undid her jeans and slid them past the flare of her rounded hips.

There was just enough light from the single street lamp in the corner of the lot for him to see the pale skin at the juncture of her thighs. Silky smooth and bare. He clenched his hands around the strap, needing to touch that warm flesh, to taste it, but knowing he couldn't move.

Beth pushed to her knees on the seat, one leg straddling his as she ran the tip of her finger up along the bare skin of her thigh. Slowly, teasing him, until her finger finally slid along her clit. She sucked in a sharp breath, her eyes closing and her head falling back. Her hips rocked against her hand, her chest rising and falling with each fast stroke of her finger.

"So fucking hot. I can see how wet you are from here. How slick that pussy is. Am I right? Tell me."

"Y-yes. Wet. So fucking wet."

Holy fuck. Wow. The unexpected word was almost as much of a turn-on as watching Beth play with herself. Adam swallowed, shifted just the tiniest bit. His cock strained, reaching, the sudden need for release almost painful in its intensity.

"Show me. Let me feel."

Beth's eyes fluttered open, her gaze resting on his. Adam held his breath, watching. Waiting. Wondering what she would do.

She slid her finger away from her clit, reached out and gently ran the wet tip along the length of his cock. Adam's body jumped to life, a long moan escaping his clenched jaw. "Fuck yes. That feels so good."

Beth muttered something, the words too soft for him to hear. And then she leaned forward and wrapped her hot mouth around his cock.

Adam's breath rushed out in a sharp hiss. His head fell back, his hips thrusting up, forcing his cock deeper into her mouth. He fought to catch his breath, released one hand from the strap and reached for her.

Beth pulled away, a teasing smile on her mouth. "I said don't let go. Put your hand back."

"Fuck. You're driving me crazy. You know that, right?" Adam raised his hand, curled it around the strap once more.

"Good." Beth's smile was teasing, sultry, hot. She kept her gaze on him as she dipped her hand between her legs, her finger stroking. Hard, fast, steady. Then she leaned forward, her mouth closing around him once more.

And fuck, she *was* driving him crazy. Sucking, licking, her mouth so fucking hot. Adam tightened his hold around the strap, worried he might rip it from the frame and snap it in two as he watched her going down on him.

As he watched her playing with herself.

He clenched his jaw, struggling for control. But fuck, this felt so good. *Beth* felt so good. Her mouth, her tongue, those sweet little sounds she was making. His hips rocked, thrusting up, over and over until he thought his entire body would instantly combust.

Beth's throaty moans grew louder, a little sharper. The nails of her free hand dug into his thigh, squeezing. Her body stiffened, going still for a heart-stopping second before she uttered a muffled scream of release, the sound vibrating around his cock.

Need for release washed over him. Swift, intense, demanding. Adam stiffened, searched for control, tried to force words from his mouth. "Beth, sweetheart, no. I'm—you have to stop—I can't—"

The ends of Beth's hair brushed across the skin of his thighs as she shook her head. Her mouth slid down the length of his cock, her tongue swirling around the tip as she cupped his balls with her hand—the same hand she had been using to stroke her clit.

Orgasm swept over him with no warning. Strong,

powerful, shattering. He expected Beth to pull away, groaned when she kept going.

Fuck. Holy fuck. Christ, her mouth was so fucking hot, hotter than the semen pulsing from his cock. Adam's eyes closed, his head fell back, his lungs struggling to draw breath as pleasure washed over him.

How long did it last? Pain, pleasure, twisting together until they were inseparable, crashing against his body until he was limp and spent. He wasn't sure how long he stayed like that, his hands still gripping the handle above him, his lungs still heaving to draw breath.

The sound of a zipper closing, of fabric brushing against fabric, seeped through the haze clouding his mind. He forced his eyes open, blinked to bring everything into focus. Beth was leaning across the front seat, reaching for her bag. Adam smiled, released his death grip on the handle, then reached out and ran his hand along her ass. She squeaked in surprise, nearly falling backward as she held the bag in front of her.

Adam pushed himself to a full sitting position then reached for her. Beth stiffened for a brief second then tilted her head up, her mouth soft under his. She pulled away too soon, averting her gaze.

"That was so fucking hot. Do you know that?"

A fleeting smile crossed her face, slightly sad. Or maybe he was just reading into things. Why would she be sad? No, he was misreading her expression, probably confusing it for embarrassment or even shyness.

Beth untangled the strap of her bag and raised it over her shoulder. Then she leaned forward, placed one hand against his cheek, and touched her lips to his. Soft, sweet. Over too fast.

"I need to go now."

Adam wanted to argue with her, to convince her to go back to his place. But she shook her head and silenced him with another quick kiss.

"I wanted to thank you. For everything."

Adam frowned. "Thank me? I don't understand."

There was no missing the sadness in her smile this time. "You don't need to." She pressed her mouth to his one last time then slid toward the door. Her hand closed around the handle and she pushed it open. Adam sat there, stunned, watching as she lowered herself to the ground, shut the door behind her, and made her way to the driver side of her own car.

Something like panic swelled inside him, dulling his reaction time. She was leaving? Just like that? And Adam knew, without a doubt, that she had just said goodbye.

Not goodnight.

Goodbye.

He struggled with his jeans, yanking them into place and quickly zipping them. Then he was scrambling across the seat, diving for the door and nearly falling out in his haste to open it.

But as fast as he was, he wasn't fast enough. Beth was already pulling out. He saw her glance to the right, watched in disbelief as she gave him a little wave and another sad smile.

And then she was gone, the car pulling out onto the main road and heading toward the interstate.

Adam stood there for several long minutes, trying to figure out what the hell had just happened.

Trying to understand the sense of loss swirling in his gut.

Chapter Sixteen

Beth followed Courtney into the break room, her steps quiet. She could have stomped into the room and Courtney probably wouldn't have heard. She was too preoccupied, lost deep in her own thoughts. Beth knew the feeling—she'd been the same way, ever since last week.

Ever since that last night with Adam.

She just hoped she was hiding it better than Courtney.

Her friend reached into a locker, dug through her purse and pulled out a bottle of aspirin, uncapping it with a shaking hand.

"You're going to give yourself an ulcer if you keep taking those. They're not good for your stomach, you know that."

She looked over her shoulder and gave Beth a small smile, then shook out three of the plain white pills. "What makes you think I don't already have an ulcer?"

"It wouldn't surprise me, as tense and jumpy as

you've been. Are you ever going to tell me what's going on?"

"Nothing's going on."

Beth snorted, the sound entirely too delicate to carry as much sarcasm as it did. She pushed away from the doorframe and stepped behind Courtney, placing her hands on her shoulders, digging her fingers into the knotted muscles. "Damn, girl. You're tighter than my last boyfriend's ass."

Courtney's eyes drifted closed and her head dropped forward. "Which boyfriend was that?"

"The firefighter." Had any of the sadness crept into her voice? She hoped not. If Courtney picked up on it, she'd asked questions—questions Beth didn't want to answer. *Couldn't* answer. Better to pretend it meant nothing.

Which was the truth.

"Adam?" Courtney raised her head, only to have Beth push it back down. "I thought you liked him."

Liked him? Beth did. Too much. That was the problem.

"I did. But he lives too far away. That, and he started looking for more than a booty call. I wasn't interested." She should be struck down by lightning for telling that lie. It so wasn't true. Not for Adam, anyway. It was what *she* had started looking for—hoping for—that scared her. But she couldn't let Courtney know that. She heaved a dramatic sigh. "But damn, I will miss that ass. And everything else he had to offer."

Courtney laughed, the sound surprised, a little foreign. Good. Courtney deserved to laugh. She'd been so quiet and withdrawn lately, so worried about…something. Beth yanked the ends of her hair and tugged her over to the small table. "Sit down if you want me to keep rubbing. You're too tall for me to do this with you standing up."

"I am not tall."

"Okay, I'm short. I said it. Are you happy?"

Courtney laughed again and settled into the hard chair, leaning forward so Beth could continue working the knots from her back. "I really thought you and Adam were going to be a thing. Don't you ever want to settle down?"

"Who, me? Nah. I'm allergic to commitment, you know that." Only because she could never find the right guy. Beth pushed against one stubborn knot, causing Courtney to hiss and hunch her shoulders. "Sorry. What about you? Don't you ever want to take a break from your self-imposed celibacy?"

"Beth! You did not just say that!"

"Sure I did. I mean, seriously. When's the last time you went out on a date?"

"I'm a single mom, it's not that easy."

"Sure it is. A guy asks you out, you say yes. Simple as that."

"No, I can't. I have Noah. You know that. And you also know that no guy would be interested in seeing a twenty-one-year-old single mother of a child with Noah's issues."

"I think you just use that as an excuse because you don't *want* to go out."

Courtney ignored the comment, just like Beth knew she would. They'd had this conversation before—too many times. Beth would try to fix her up with someone, try to talk her into going out. Courtney always said no. That wasn't her life right now. It had never been her life.

"So you never did tell me how you and the hot

firefighter met."

"Trying to change the subject, hm? Fine, I won't bring up your serious lack of a social life again. For now. And I'm seriously not telling you how we met."

"Why not?"

"Because it might offend your virginal sensibilities, that's why." Offend? Courtney would have a heart attack. Literally. Then she'd lecture Beth on the dangers of meeting strangers, especially for the sake of having sex.

And she'd be right. Even Adam had warned her, telling her it was dangerous. That's why she hadn't gone back to the chatroom, not once.

At least, that's what she told herself. She wasn't ready to admit that she didn't want to go back. She wasn't interested in meeting anyone else. Wasn't interested in hooking up with anyone else.

And she didn't want to risk seeing Adam in there. She wasn't ready for that, wasn't ready to admit that seeing him there, knowing he was hooking up with someone else, would hurt.

Stupid. So stupid. They didn't have a relationship—they never did, no matter what Beth may have told Courtney. She was never going to see Adam again. She couldn't, it was a risk she couldn't afford to take, not when she realized it was starting to be about more than sex.

For her, at least.

Courtney hunched her shoulders together and glanced back at Beth. "I am hardly virginal. I have a kid, remember?"

Beth laughed, the short sound holding a world of sarcasm and disbelief. "Okay. So you had sex. Once. Over three years ago. I'm so impressed."

Courtney opened her mouth, no doubt to disagree, then snapped her mouth closed again. Beth almost felt sorry for her. She knew Noah was Courtney's whole life. Knew that being a single mother wasn't easy, that Courtney struggled to find what she thought was the right balance. But her friend deserved happiness, deserved to find that someone special.

One of them had to. It should be Courtney. She deserved it. She deserved so much more. But Beth could sense her discomfort, knew she wasn't ready. Maybe she never would be. And Courtney would never admit it, but Beth was certain it had something to do with Noah's father—whoever he was. Beth knew better than to ask about him again so she forced a laugh, decided that Courtney needed a little teasing.

"No come back, hm?"

"I know better."

Beth made a little humming noise under her breath and kept working on the tense muscles under her hand. Courtney leaned forward even more, releasing her breath and letting herself relax. The music piped into the salon's speakers was muted back here, nothing more than a backdrop for the other sounds surrounding them. The chatter of conversation between stylist and client was nothing more than a relaxing buzz, lulling her deeper into a foggy gray world. The phone rang from somewhere out on the floor; the bell signaling the arrival or departure of another client was nothing more than a barely-heard tinkle.

In a few minutes, she'd have to get back up. Go to work with her next client, shampooing and cutting. But for now, for these few precious minutes, she could help her friend relax and do her best to put Adam from her mind. It was easier, at least a little bit, to focus on helping Courtney deal with her problems.

Whatever they were.

"Your purple is fading."

"Hm?"

"I said your purple is fading." Beth reached up and grabbed the ends of Courtney's hair, separated out a thick strand. "You should change it."

Courtney sighed and straightened, reaching back to pull her hair from Beth's hand. "I happen to like the purple."

"I know you do. But Fall's here. New season, new color. I'm thinking you'd look really good with some red."

"Red? I don't think so—"

"Not *red* red. More like an auburn cinnamon. With highlights. That would really make your color pop."

"What's wrong with my color?"

"Nothing. Except you've been so stressed lately that you're super pale. The blonde only makes you look more washed out."

"Oh, and going red would be any better?"

"Sure. A nice warm color, nothing too drastic." Beth started running her fingers through her hair, pulling strands in different directions. "We've never done a red on you before. I think it'll look good."

"I don't know. Maybe."

"No maybes about it. I already know what I'm going to do. Can you stay late tonight? I'll do it then—"

"Hey Courtney, someone's here to see you."

They both turned toward Shelly, another stylist. There was something about the other woman's expression that made Courtney tense, made her hands curl into fists. This wasn't about a client, Beth knew that as surely as Courtney did.

A man stood behind Shelly, middle-aged in a dark, nondescript suit. Everything about him was nondescript. Average, unassuming. Someone you'd pass on the street and not even notice.

So why did he fill Courtney with so much obvious fear and dread? And why did Beth suddenly place a hand on her shoulder, offering her friend support?

"Miss Williams?"

"Y-yes?"

The man pushed past Shelly, a white envelope held in his hand. He stopped in front of Courtney, his face blank of all expression, and held the envelope out to her. "This is a request for a paternity test on one Noah Robert Williams. The information on where to have the test taken is inside. I would suggest you not ignore it."

"What?" The word fell from Courtney's mouth in a strangled whisper. It didn't matter, the man was already walking out. Beth's hand tightened on her shoulder and she leaned closer, peering at the envelope in Courtney's shaking hand.

Courtney looked down at it, her eyes dazed, almost as if she didn't see it. She squeezed her eyes closed, opened them, blinked a few times. Beth looked over her shoulder, her gaze falling on the return address so crisply printed in the corner. It was from a law firm.

"Courtney! Oh my God. What is it? Open it! What did he mean? Paternity? For Noah? Why? For what?" Beth's questions came one after the other, the words nothing more than senseless sound. Courtney probably didn't even hear them. She looked lost, frightened.

Scared to death.

She dropped the envelope onto the table and pushed her chair back, nearly knocking Beth over. "Throw it in the trash. I don't want it."

"Shelly, grab me a bottle of water." Beth bent down next to her and placed a comforting hand on her leg. Her other hand snagged the envelope from the table and held it between them. "Courtney, I don't think you can ignore this. You heard him. You need to open it."

"No. No, I don't."

"Courtney, he sounded serious. You need to open it."

"I can't."

"You have to. But I don't understand, why would anyone want a paternity test on Noah? I thought you said you knew who his father was."

"I did. I do." She closed her eyes, bit down on her trembling lower lip. All the color drained from her face, leaving her pale. Her hands started shaking. Her whole body was shaking, her chest rising and falling with each short gasp. Beth worried that she might actually pass out. She'd never seen Courtney look like this, so...terrified.

She shifted in the chair, finally opened her eyes and rested her frantic gaze on Beth. "Open it for me. I can't. I don't want—you have to open it."

Beth watched her for a long minute, a hundred different unasked questions flashing through her mind. Then she nodded and slowly opened the envelope, surprised to see her own fingers shaking. She pulled out a single sheet of paper, the letterhead matching the name of the law firm on the envelope.

Beth looked at Courtney once more, silently

asking permission to read it. Courtney nodded, her eyes fixed on Beth as she skimmed the several short paragraphs.

"What does it say?"

"It's a bunch of legal jargon." Beth frowned, her eyes skimming the page once more. "Something about something called an Acknowledgement of Paternity to establish—ohmygod. I know this name. Holy shit. Oh. My. God. Courtney! Seriously? *He's* Noah's father? Holy shit, I don't believe it."

Courtney snatched the paper from Beth's shaking hand and read it for herself.

Had Beth read the name correctly? She had. But she still couldn't believe it. No wonder Courtney never talked about Noah's father. Harland Day had been a hockey player, a local boy made good who made it to the professionals. He'd played for the Baltimore Banners up until last season, when he was sent back here to their minor affiliate in York.

There had been rumors and stories floating around about him. About his partying. About his escapades with different women. God, no wonder Courtney looked so scared. No wonder she didn't want him in Noah's life. Beth couldn't blame her.

Unless—maybe he *wanted* to be in Noah's life. Maybe the stories had been just that: stories.

And maybe Beth needed to stop dreaming. Needed to learn how to be more realistic, like Courtney.

"Is he really Noah's father?"

Courtney folded the letter and carefully tucked it back into the envelope, refusing to look at Beth. "Yes."

"You? And Harland Day? But—"

"It was a long time ago, okay? I don't like thinking

about it."

"How can you *not* think about it? He's Noah's father!"

"And he didn't even know about Noah until a few weeks ago! I don't know why he's doing this. It makes no sense—"

"But isn't this a good thing? I mean, it looks like he *wants* to be named as Noah's father. That means you can get him to pay child support and help—"

"No!" Courtney jumped from the chair and started pacing around the small room, her arms wrapped tightly around her middle. They had an audience now: Shelly and Diane and Jackie crowded together in the doorway, their expressions ranging from concern to blatant curiosity.

Courtney paused her frantic pacing, glanced at the women huddled in the doorway, then turned back to Beth. "I don't want his money. I don't want his help. I don't want anything to do with him and I don't want him in our lives."

"But why? Wouldn't this help—"

"Because he accused me of sleeping with someone else when I first told him I was pregnant. He kept insisting, over and over and over, that the baby wasn't his. That it couldn't be his." Courtney made an angry swipe at the tears running down her face. "So I told him it wasn't. I told him I wouldn't have it and that was it. I never saw him again."

"Oh, Courtney." Beth hurried over to her and pulled her into a comforting hug. Several more pairs of arms joined them, offering words of comfort and consolation and support. Beth didn't know how long they stood there, huddled together. She pulled away, wiped her own face, her mouth trembling with a watery smile.

"Okay, no more of this. Shelly, you and the others get back out there. Diane, can you take Courtney's next appointment?"

"Sure, no problem."

"I can take my own appointment." Courtney tried to object but Beth waved her off before shooing everyone out of the room. "Beth, I can take—"

"No, you can't." She grabbed the envelope from the table and held it out. "You need to get this taken care of first."

Courtney stepped back and shook her head. "No. I want nothing to do with that."

"Courtney, you can't ignore it."

"I'm not letting them put more needles in Noah. I'm not. Not for this. I don't care what they say."

"Then go talk to his father."

"Beth, I told you, I don't want—"

"This isn't going to go away, no matter how much you want it to. You should at least go talk to him. Maybe there's another way. Maybe there's some way to work this out so you're *both* happy."

Happy? Did Beth really believe this would end happily? She had to, one way or another. Courtney deserved it. Out of everyone here, Courtney deserved it the most.

She stared down at the envelope in Beth's outstretched hand, eyeing it with distaste and fear. Then she reluctantly took it, a look of stunned surprise crossing her face. Her hand tightened around the letter, partially crumpling it. Then she raised her head and looked at Beth, fear clear in her eyes. "I don't know what to do."

"Go talk to him. It's the only thing you *can* do for

now."

She hoped Beth would take the advice, hoped it would work out better for her friend than it had for her.

Not that talking to Adam would help in her situation. How could it? There was nothing to talk about.

Chapter Seventeen

Adam stretched his legs out and rested his head against the back of the bench. Warmth from the evening sun bathed his face as faint orange light seeped between his closed lids. Echoes of light traffic coming from the interstate behind the station floated through the air, nothing more than a faint hum occasionally broken by the louder roar of a diesel engine.

He had come out here for peace and quiet, for a chance to just clear his mind and get away from the bickering going on in the kitchen. He wasn't interested in the hockey game they were watching on television. Wasn't interested in deciding what to have for dinner or where to go this coming weekend.

Wasn't interested in anything except trying to clear his fucking mind until he stopped seeing a shy smile whenever he closed his eyes.

Why the fuck did his mind insist on dredging up images of Beth every time he closed his eyes? Every night when he went home, every night when he fell asleep. Every fucking time he turned on his computer and thought about logging into the chatroom. He never got past entering his username and password, told himself it was because he wasn't interested in hooking up, that he just needed a break for a little bit.

Tried to convince himself it had nothing to do with the gut-wrenching fear of seeing Beth in there. Of knowing that she might be looking for her own hook-up.

One that didn't include him.

He sucked in a deep breath and wrapped his hands around the edge of the bench. Wood, hard and rough, dug into his palms, almost painful.

Still not enough to get those fucking images from his mind.

What the fuck was wrong with him? Why the fuck couldn't he stop thinking about her? He shouldn't be giving her any more thought than what he spared his other hook-ups. So why was he? Why hadn't he been able to think of anything else for the last two weeks?

Because of the way she left him. That had to be it. He'd never had that happen before, not like that. She'd gone down on him, sucked him off, and then just...left.

His mind balked at the vulgarity and he wasn't sure why because that's exactly what happened.

Except it wasn't. Not really. Not in Beth's case. She deserved more than vulgar references, more than the lewdness of a casual memory.

But *why*? What the fuck was so different about Beth? Why had she gotten to him? It didn't make sense.

And that's what worried the fuck out of him.

"You're going to get splinters if you don't let up on that bench."

Adam jumped at the quiet warning. He released

his hold on the bench and sat up, darting a quick glance at Mikey. Great, just what he needed. Didn't she know he wanted to be left alone in peace and quiet so he could wallow in his own misery and self-pity?

Obviously not. Or, if she did, she didn't care. She stepped closer, leaned down and swatted his leg. "Why do all of you guys always insist on sitting in the middle and taking up all the room? Scoot over."

Adam's sigh was filled with impatience, letting her know he wasn't in the mood for company. Mikey didn't care because she lowered herself on the bench next to him then shoved him to the side with her hip.

"Mikey, I'm not in the mood."

"No shit. And too bad."

Adam grunted. Fine, whatever. She could sit there all she wanted. That didn't mean he had to talk to her.

"I'm surprised to see you out here. Figured you'd be in the back, studying."

"I needed a break."

"For the last two tricks?"

"I'm studying at home." Except he wasn't. He wasn't doing anything at home except sitting there, staring into space.

"The test is in a month."

"I know."

"Are you going to be ready for it?"

"I'll be ready." Adam tilted his head to the side and fixed her with a steady glare. "The question is, will *you* be ready?"

"Me?" Mikey shook her head, her ponytail swinging behind her with the motion. "I'm not taking it."

"Why the hell not? I thought you were."

"Changed my mind."

"Fuck, Mikey. Why? You'd ace that exam. And you'd make a great lieutenant."

She shrugged and looked away but not before he saw the frown cross her face—or the contradicting smile that briefly lifted the corners of her mouth. "Maybe next year."

"Bullshit. What changed your mind? You were all gung-ho about it six months ago when the notice came out."

"Shit happens. You know that. And I didn't come out here to talk about me—I came out here to talk about *you*. What the hell are you moping around for?"

"I'm not."

"Yeah? My turn to call bullshit. What's going on?"

"Nothing is going on. I'm just trying to clear my mind, get ready for the test."

"Yeah, sure you are. You know you're not fooling anyone, right?"

"Ask me if I care."

Mikey laughed and shook her head. "Why do I have the feeling the problem is that you care too much?"

"Not me. You know better than that."

Mikey pinned him with a glare, her mossy green eyes steady, seeing too much. Silence stretched between them, long enough that Adam started to squirm. He looked away, breaking the intense eye contact, wondering what Mikey had seen when she watched him so closely.

Afraid she saw too much.

"You're right. I do."

Adam stared straight ahead, his gaze focused on the bare trees lining the ramp leading out to the road. "You do, what?"

"Know you better than that. We all do. Hell, Adam. How long have we all worked together? There aren't any secrets here. You know that."

"Great. Wonderful. That doesn't mean I need anyone all up in my business. Including you. Even if there are no secrets."

"Actually, there's one secret nobody knows about yet."

Adam heard the hesitancy in her voice, sensed the confusion in her words. He looked over at her, saw the way her brows were pulled low over her eyes, noticed the way she chewed on her lower lip, as if she was worried about something.

Adam told himself not to ask, tried to convince himself he didn't care. This was just Mikey, being melodramatic—no doubt to get him to open up and talk.

Except Mikey didn't do melodrama. Mikey was the steadiest and most even-keeled person he knew.

"Okay, fine. What secret is that?"

A faint smile flashed across her face. "I'll tell if you tell."

"Yeah, right. Bullshit. Nice try but it's not going to work. You should know better—"

"I'm pregnant."

Adam stared at her, not sure he heard the whispered words correctly. She had to be joking. Had to be pulling his leg. No way was she serious. This had to be nothing more than a ploy to get him to open up.

Only she didn't look like she was joking. She looked…worried. Excited. Scared.

"Are you fucking serious?"

"As a heart attack."

"Really?"

"Yeah, Adam. Really. You think I would make a fucking joke about something like this?"

"No. I—no." He pulled a deep breath in through his nose and quickly released it. "Is, uh, is this a good thing?"

"Yeah." Mikey frowned, nodded. Held still for a long second and nodded again. "Yeah, it's good. Unexpected, though."

"Good. Good, then. Congratulations." He draped his arm around her shoulders and pulled her in for a quick hug.

"Yeah, thanks." She pulled away and leaned forward, tucked her hands under her legs and stared straight ahead. "Nobody knows yet. Not even Jay. You can't tell a soul. I mean it, Adam. I don't want anyone to know yet."

"Mikey, you have to tell them. You can't keep working—"

"I'm only two months along. The doctor said I was fine, that I can keep working for a little while longer. And SOP says I can stay out in the field until I'm six months along."

"Bullshit. We both know that's not safe, I don't give a flying fuck what standard operating procedure says."

"Yeah, I know. I, uh, I'll probably go on light duty next month." She turned back to him, her face serious. "I mean it, Adam. You can't tell anyone."

"I won't."

She studied him for a quiet minute then finally nodded, satisfied that he was telling the truth. Another minute went by then she grinned and nudged him in the side. "Okay, I told you my secret. Now tell me what the hell is going on with you. It's about that girl you've been seeing, isn't it? Beth?"

Adam opened his mouth before he had a chance to decide what to tell her. Was he going to deny it? Or was he going to open up about it?

He never got a chance one way or the other because the alarm blared to life, a loud screech that broke the silence around them. They jumped from the bench in unison, ran inside as the dispatcher's disembodied voice announced a dwelling fire. Adam scrambled into his gear and raced for the engine, climbing in behind Pete as Mikey raced around to the other side. Dale put the engine in gear, pulling out with a roar as Pete hit the siren.

He could smell it before they turned onto the street: that particular odor of smoke, heavy and thick with wood and plastic and everything else imaginable. He turned, saw the crowd of onlookers standing near the curb, saw heavy black smoke coming from the third story of the large house.

They moved in unison, no words needed as he and Mikey pulled the line and dragged it toward the house while Pete assessed the scene, talking into his radio.

Dale charged the line, the hiss of water loud as Mikey and Adam secured their facemasks in place. Mikey grabbed the nozzle and hurried forward, Adam right behind her, humping hose as they advanced inside and up the stairs.

Something was wrong. Something felt...off. It was too hot, too thick. They needed ventilation, fast. How soon before the truck company got here? Minutes, no longer than that.

They reached the third floor, the heat intensifying as they moved forward. He could just make out the deep glow of red, like a monster's eye staring out at them from a hood of black.

"Hit it!" His voice was muffled by the facemask, the sound reminding him of something from a sci-fi movie. He could barely see Mikey, even though his face was damn near plastered against her ass. But he didn't have to see to know she was shaking her head.

"Not yet. Closer."

"Bullshit, Mikey. Hit it."

She muttered something he couldn't make out, figured she was probably cussing him out. He heard the hiss of water, felt it rush to life through the hose line as she opened the nozzle.

Heat, searing and painful, wrapped around them. Steam—but something else, too. Something...not right. Adam didn't know if he heard it—or if he sensed it. Something, some faint warning or instinct or sense of foreboding. He didn't know, just reacted at the same time Mikey did.

Too late.

A deafening roar, an explosion of red and orange, an inferno of heat. Adam reached for Mikey, wrapped his arms around her and pulled her close, tried to roll with her. Protecting her, trying to shelter her. Thinking of the life she carried inside her, thinking she'd probably cuss him out when they got back to the station.

They were spinning. Flying. Falling.

And then the world went black.

Chapter Eighteen

Pain. Searing, burning. His gut twisted with it, turning inside out. Adam sucked in a deep breath, felt pain explode in his chest, cried out against it.

He struggled to sit up but he couldn't move, his body was too heavy. Something was holding him down. So much fucking pain.

He tried to force his eyes open, closed them against the bright lights flashing overhead. Heaven? No, no fucking way. Not with this much pain.

Hell, then. No less than he deserved for his sins. No less than what his black soul called for.

No. Not yet. He wasn't ready. There was something he needed to do, something—

He struggled against the pain, screaming as his insides twisted and tried to rebel. He reached out, his hands searching wildly, touching nothing as pain wracked his body. He wasn't ready to die, not yet. Not when there was something he needed—

"Adam, calm down. Stop struggling. You're going to rip the fucking IV out of your arm or puncture a lung."

That voice. Deep, forceful, filled with authority. He knew that voice. From where? Who? Other noises filtered through. Loud, mechanical. More voices. Strange ones. Shouts. Words he couldn't make out, didn't understand.

"Adam, listen to me. We're moving you off the stretcher. This might hurt, buddy."

Hurt? No, nothing could hurt, not more than it already did.

He was wrong.

Every inch of his body screamed in pain. He could *feel* the sound, ripping from the pores of his skin, the noise surrounding him, harsh and raspy. He was floating, but only for seconds before his body crashed against…something.

And then he was still. Unmoving. For the space of a blissful second, he felt nothing. And then his body screamed again, pain shooting through his chest and shoulder and back.

He wanted it to stop. Needed it to stop. Fuck, what the hell was wrong with him? What the fuck had happened?

He struggled, ignored the pain in his chest as he fought to get his eyes open. As he fought to breathe, fought against the drowning sensation.

"Dammit, Price, knock it the fuck off."

That voice again. He *knew* it. But how?

He finally peeled his eyes open, looked up into the blurry image of a face. Blinked, blinked again, trying to focus. Dark hair. Brown eyes. Stern jaw and mouth pressed into a tight line.

A name floated through his mind, just out of reach. Adam clenched his jaw, struggled to grab the name from where it floated in front of him, hovering, teasing him.

Dave.

Yes, that was right. Dave. Dave Warren, their paramedic.

More names flooded his brain, swirling around with dizzying speed. An image, dark, thick, red and black.

Adam tried to swallow, tried to focus. He needed to *focus* dammit, needed to remember...there was something, just there, out of reach. Something important.

"Hang on, Adam. They're going to sedate you. You'll be flying high in no time."

"No." He shouted the word, only nobody heard him. His throat hurt, his mouth too dry and parched. He inhaled, felt stabbing pain shoot through him, ignored it. Struggled against that odd drowning sensation. "No."

And then he remembered. The heat. The fire. The explosion. The darkness. He tried to push up on his elbows, struggled against the hold on his arm as he shook his head.

"No. Mikey. Where—"

"She's right behind us. She's fine. Now stop fucking moving."

Relief swept through him, short-lived as another wave of pain crashed over him. His body stiffened, trying to fight against it, trying to distance himself from it. More voices, lower, softer. He didn't understand the words, didn't need to. He just needed the pain to stop, just for a minute. That's all he needed.

Just for a minute.

"Hang in there, Adam. Just a few more minutes."

A few more minutes? For what? He didn't know, didn't care. He just needed the pain to stop.

Needed something. No…someone.

Needed…

#

Black. Cool, comforting.

No, not black. It was fading, growing lighter. He didn't want it to get lighter, knew that something was waiting for him, something he didn't want to face. He struggled, tried to force his body back into the blackness.

Too weak, he couldn't fight it, didn't have the strength. Could only watch as the black turned to gray, as the gray grew paler, lightening, growing.

He sucked in a deep breath, groaned as red-hot pain seared his chest, tried to gulp in air, fought against the strange drowning sensation. Something closed over his arm, the touch cool, soothing. Comforting.

"Beth?"

A quiet laugh filled the silence surrounding him. Soft, tired. Strained. He knew that laugh, recognized it but couldn't put a name to it, couldn't put a face to it.

"No, asshole. It's Mikey."

Mikey. Images floated through his mind, scattered and disjointed. He watched, oddly detached, as they swirled around, finally falling into place like pieces of a giant puzzle.

Sitting on a bench, talking.

An alarm shattering the silence.

The fire. That feeling that something wasn't right. Heat, intense and searing. And then…

Nothing.

Adam struggled to open his eyes, fought against the heaviness of his lids until they finally listened. Dim light made him blink, blink again until the burning sensation faded away.

He turned his head, his gaze focusing on the woman beside him. Long hair, mussed and shaggy. Dark green eyes, rimmed in red and framed with dark circles. Dirt smeared the pale face. No, not dirt. Soot. Black smears along her cheek and one side of her jaw, faded and spotty, like they hadn't been completely washed away. A small bruise, black and purple, covered the other side of her face.

Adam closed his eyes, exhaled, winced as pain shot through his chest. "You look like shit."

Another laugh, just as soft as the first one. "I look like a beauty queen compared to you."

Adam grunted, peeled his eyes open again and turned his head. "What the fuck happened?"

"What happened?" Mikey tried to smile, her lips quivering. She reached up with one shaking hand, ran it across both watery eyes. "You had to go and get all macho and be a fucking gentleman. That's what happened."

Adam grunted again and turned away, tried to swallow against the thickness clogging his throat. "So you owe me."

"Yeah, guess I do."

"You okay?"

"Yeah." Her voice broke. She cleared her throat, her hand tightening ever so briefly on his arm. "For the most part."

"The baby—"

"Is fine, too."

"Then what—"

"Broken ankle. I was discharged yesterday."

"Yesterday?"

"Yeah. You've been out of it." She hesitated, finally removed her hand from his arm. Adam heard her move, heard the quick hiss that escaped her as she shifted. He peeled his eyes open again, turned his head to look at her.

"What happened?"

"You remember any of it?"

Adam frowned, trying to put the last pieces of the puzzle together in his mind. No matter how hard he tried, they wouldn't quite fit. "Some. Parts of it. Not everything."

"It flashed. The floor collapsed and we fell through. You, uh, you took the brunt of it."

"Feels like it."

She laughed again, the sound strained, fading away into the artificial silence of the room. Adam closed his eyes, exhaustion sweeping over him. The blackness was calling him again, beckoning him with its peaceful nothingness.

Not yet. He needed to know, needed to ask...

"How bad?"

"What?"

Adam swallowed, kept his eyes closed against whatever he might see on Mikey's face. "Burnt. How bad?"

He couldn't feel anything, nothing more than the steady sharpness of pain in his chest and shoulder. That didn't mean anything, though. And he had to know.

Fear shot through him with Mikey's silence. Sharp, bitter, eclipsing the pain he felt. Fuck. His biggest fear, staring him in the face. Maybe it was a blessing he couldn't feel it, maybe he shouldn't have asked. He swallowed again, tried to force a smile to his face. "That bad, huh?"

"You're not."

Adam pried open one eye and looked at her, certain he had heard wrong. "I'm not?"

"No. Is that what you thought?"

"Yeah. Felt like it. Earlier. My chest. My back. My shoulder. Everything. Burning."

"Well, you're not. I mean, nothing more than a few blisters here and there." Mikey's hand wrapped around his, squeezing.

"Then why the hell does my body hurt so much?"

"You sure you want to know?"

"Is it that bad?"

"Depends on your point of view, I guess. Hope you were looking forward to an extended paid vacation."

"Just—" He took a quick breath, winced, released it. The blackness was calling him again, its pull not quite as strong. He still fought against it. Just a few more minutes, that's all he needed. "Tell me."

Mikey was quiet for so long, he didn't think she was going to answer. Her shoulders heaved with a deep breath, sagged when she blew it out. "You broke your collarbone. Two ribs on your left side. Punctured your lung."

"No wonder it hurts to breathe."

"Yeah. Ha ha. Real funny." She wiped a hand across her eyes and offered him a smile that quickly died. "You, uh, you punctured the lung when they were bringing you in. Dave said—you, uh, you were fighting them. Asking about...about me."

He didn't remember that. Or did he? Images

flashed in the back of his mind, fuzzy. Fast. Maybe he remembered. He remembered Dave, yelling at him. Remembered searing pain. That awful sensation that he was drowning. And then...nothing.

Did it matter that he couldn't remember? He didn't think so. Didn't care enough to worry about it.

Adam stared up at the ceiling, trying to pinpoint the different areas of pain. It didn't work, not when his entire body from the waist up was throbbing with it, a dull ache that was growing sharper with each passing minute. "Anything else?"

"Yeah. You've got one hell of a bruise on your back from landing on the bottle."

"Probably from you landing on top of me."

"Yeah. Probably." Mikey's voice cracked, the sound thick and strangled. Adam turned his head to the side, felt his gut twist when he saw the single tear trailing down Mikey's cheek. He twisted his arm, hissed in pain, quickly changed position as his hand found hers and squeezed. "Fuck, Mikey. Don't do that. I can't handle that."

"Screw you. It's hormones." She wiped her hand across her eyes once more. Adam tightened his hold around her hand, tugged until she leaned forward. He gave her an awkward hug, tried to pat her on the back before she pulled away with a sniffle. "I'm fine."

"Good. Now get the hell out of here and let me sleep."

"Not yet. I'm staying until they kick me out. Don't worry, it won't be too long. I think you're due for more painkillers soon."

"Good."

His eyes drifted closed, his mind searching for the darkness. It was farther away now, hovering just out of reach. Maybe, if he concentrated hard enough, if he willed it closer—

"Oh. One more thing." Mikey's voice, steadier now, pulled him back just before he could reach it. He swallowed back a groan and looked at her.

"What?"

"You're going to probably need a haircut."

"What?"

Mikey shifted in the chair—a wheelchair, he finally noticed—and bit back a quick smile. Her gaze darted to his head then skipped away. "Yeah. You, uh, might have singed some of those surfer waves you were always flaunting."

Adam grunted, grimaced in pain, let out a quick breath. "It was time for a new cut anyway."

"Good. I happen to know someone who does just that."

"No. Don't even go there, Mikey. Not happening."

"You were calling her name. You know that, right?"

"No."

"Well, you were. She'd probably want to know."

"No."

"Why do you have to be so fucking bullheaded? You could have died. You know that, right? We both could have."

"We didn't."

Mikey made a sound, a cross between a growl and a hiss. She leaned forward, opened her mouth to say something, snapped it shut again and blew out a heavy sigh. "You're an ass."

"No shit." He closed his eyes, willed the blackness to come back. He wanted to disappear, to be engulfed in the dark nothingness where he could just float. Where nothing else mattered.

Only the darkness was gone, yanked away when Mikey squeezed his hand again. He muttered an oath and forced his eyes open. "You're a pain in my fucking ass."

"Yeah. I know." One corner of her mouth curled up, the half-smile strained, forced. "I like her, Adam. I think you do, too."

"No."

"Why?"

"She deserves better than me, Mikey. We both know that."

The hand tightened around his, almost painful. "Bullshit. Why do you say shit like that?"

"Nothing but the truth." God, he didn't want to talk about this now. He was tired, so fucking tired. His eyes drifted closed, waiting, praying for the darkness to come back.

"You're too hard on yourself."

"Let it go, Mikey. We both know the shit I've done. She deserves better."

"You don't believe that. You can't. I just want—"

She was interrupted by a nurse walking in, an older woman with a stern face and a take-no-prisoners attitude resting on her slim shoulders. She looked at Mikey then moved closer to the bed, reaching for the IV line dangling from his arm, right above the grip Mikey had on his hand. Funny, he hadn't noticed it before.

"How's the pain?"

"It's there."

The nurse's mouth twitched in what might have been a smile. She pulled a needle out, uncapped it, plunged it into the IV line then patted his hand. "It won't be in a little bit."

Adam nodded, let his eyes drift closed. Numbness spread over him, the grayness surrounding him growing darker, beckoning him, pulling him into its embrace. Soothing, comforting. The nothingness waited for him, calling him.

He heard his name, soft and far away, nothing more than a faint echo. Something squeezed his hand as the disembodied voice floated around him, following him into the soothing darkness.

You need her, Adam.

Chapter Nineteen

Adam's hurt.
Hospital.
Accident at work.
Not critical.

Beth clenched the steering wheel, her grip so tight that her fingers started cramping. Her mouth opened, sucked in a huge gulping breath of air. She needed to calm down, to slow down. Getting into an accident because she was flying down the interstate wouldn't help anything.

She hadn't been calm since she received the text messages early this afternoon. The only thing that had stopped her from frantically racing out the door of the salon was that last one, telling her he wasn't critical.

She had almost ignored the text messages at first, wondering if someone had the wrong number, if someone was texting her by mistake. She hadn't seen Adam since their last night more than two weeks ago, when she'd said goodbye. She didn't recognize the incoming number, only knew that it was a Maryland area code. Surely the texts weren't for her; they must be meant for someone else.

That didn't stop the sharp pain of worry that ripped through her when she saw them. There had been nothing between them, nothing more than sex. Yet the idea of Adam being hurt, of that beautiful, vital body being injured, filled her with pain and fear and...

She shook her head and wiped a shaking hand across her eyes. Nothing more than sex? Who was she kidding? Somehow, somewhere along the way, she had started thinking of Adam as something more than a casual encounter. Oh God, how had she let it happen? It shouldn't have...but it did.

It was for that reason she almost ignored the text messages. They hadn't been meant for her—they couldn't be. But she received a few more, calling her by name.

Beth finally learned that the sender was Mikey, the woman firefighter from Adam's shift. A woman she had only briefly spoken to, a woman she barely knew.

It was the final message that had sent her running from the salon in something close to panic.

He needs you, Beth, only he doesn't know it.

Stupid. God, she was so stupid. Why was she racing to the hospital on the word of one of Adam's co-workers? This was a mistake, a huge mistake that would only result in heartbreak. She doubted that Adam needed her—she doubted he needed anyone. She was flying down the interstate, breaking the speed limit and risking an accident, to go see a man who didn't even know she was coming.

A man who would no doubt be very surprised when she showed up. And he probably wasn't even hurt that bad. She was probably overreacting and imagining the worst.

Her foot eased off the accelerator as she merged off I83 toward the exit for Charles Street, her phone's map app telling her to stay to the right. An overwhelming urge to turn the car around and go back home washed over her. Yes, she was overreacting. This was a mistake that would end in embarrassment for both of them.

But what if she wasn't overreacting?

It was that very slim possibility that kept her driving in the direction of the hospital.

South along Charles Street, past something that looked like an old castle on her left. Traffic slowed in front of her, stopping for a light. Her phone instructed her to turn left onto Towsontown Boulevard, to make a right onto Osler Drive. She drove through parts of a university campus, finally turning left onto Sister Pierre Drive to the hospital entrance.

She pulled into the parking garage and eased the old car into an empty space on the third level. And then she sat there, her forehead resting against the steering wheel, wondering if she was making a big mistake.

Her heart pounded in her chest, her breathing shaky and too fast. Yes, this was a mistake. She would walk into the room and see the unwelcome surprise on Adam's face and realize he had no desire to see her.

But what if she saw something else?

Foolish. So foolish.

She was here. She'd just go in, say hi, and that would be it. Five minutes, no more than that. Just enough to say hi and to reassure herself that he was fine and then she'd turn around and leave. She'd come this far, after all, she might as well see it through.

And it wasn't like this would be the first time she'd

made a fool of herself in front of a man. One more time wouldn't hurt her.

She grabbed her purse and climbed out of the car, choosing to ignore the tiny little voice that piped up and called her a liar. The heels of her short boots clicked on the concrete as she walked toward the elevator. Just a few minutes, that was all. She could survive a few minutes.

She entered the hospital, paused as she looked around the lobby. Mikey had given her Adam's room number. Did she need to check in at a desk, or just go up? She wasn't sure.

Better safe than sorry.

She pulled the straps of her purse higher on her shoulder and made her way to the elderly man sitting at the desk. He looked up at her with kind eyes, an expectant smile on his face.

"I'm—I'm here to see Adam Price." Beth gave him the room number and waited. The man entered something into the computer then asked her to sign in as he gave her a visitor's badge. Beth clipped it to the collar of her sweater then started toward another set of elevators. Her gaze swept past a small gift store and she hesitated.

She shouldn't, not really.

But now that she saw it, she realized she wanted to. Just something small, maybe even something silly.

Ten minutes later, she was on the elevator leading up to Adam's floor, a single helium balloon attached to the hand of a small stuffed bear dressed in firefighter gear. She was already regretting the purchase, thought about leaving the silly thing behind in the elevator when the doors opened with a small hiss.

She was already making a fool of herself by

coming to see him, she might as well go all the way. It was just a stupid bear that meant nothing. No harm in giving it to him.

She stepped off the elevator, studied the signs on the wall across from her, then turned left. The maze of hallways stretched around her, leading in different directions. She had to backtrack twice, looking for the right wing. A nurse took pity on her and pointed her in the right direction, her smile widening at the sight of the bear and balloon.

At least someone appreciated it.

Beth tugged on the heavy wooden doors, entered another hallway lined with rooms. The noise of mechanical beeps and groans and soft conversation hummed around her, oddly hushed. She heard laughter coming from a room at the end of the hall, out of place, almost jarring. Under the laughter was another voice, a little deeper, strained and somehow forced. A nurse came out of one room, frowned in the direction of the noise, then finally noticed Beth standing there. Her gaze lowered to the bear in Beth's hands then she pointed in the direction where the laughter had come from.

"Last room on your right."

Sweat dampened Beth's hands and she wondered how the nurse knew which room she was looking for. The firefighter bear, it must be. She headed in that direction, scanning each room number just in case. She didn't want to enter a stranger's room by mistake.

She didn't want to enter Adam's room, either, not when she saw the people crowded in there. Nobody had noticed her yet, it wasn't too late. She could still leave without embarrassing herself.

A head turned as she started backing away from

the door. Piercing gray eyes caught hers, flared with recognition. The man—his name was Jay—nudged the man next to him. Conversation slowly died away as more heads turned, one by one, to look at her.

Beth tightened her grip on the bear and almost ran off under all the scrutiny—but her feet were glued to the floor, unable to move. She swallowed, the sound loud in her ears, and scanned the faces. Most of them were familiar. At least, she thought they were. She wasn't really looking at them, she was trying to see the bed—but it was hidden behind the bodies of Adam's other visitors.

Beth shifted, wondered if she looked as frightened as she felt. This had been a mistake. A huge mistake.

She wondered if it was too late to back out of the room, too late to run down the hall and out to her car. She took one hesitant step back, ready to do just that, when the crowd moved away from the bed and she got her first glimpse of Adam.

And oh God, had that strangled gasp come from her? It must have, the way everyone was looking at her. She closed her mouth, pressed her lips into a tight line, ignored the sudden wave of dizziness that washed over her. The man in the bed didn't look like Adam, not at first.

A white sheet covered him from the waist down, the color somehow washing out the bare skin of his abdomen. His right arm was held in place against his bare chest with some kind of sling. She could see a tube of some kind sticking out from under his arm. Oh God, the tube had been inserted into his chest, she could see where it entered his skin and was held in place with white tape. Another tube ran from his left arm, up through some kind of machine and into a clear bag suspended from a hook above his bed. An oxygen mask rested at an odd angle near his pale face. Beth could hear the slight hiss of air and wondered briefly why it wasn't covering his mouth and nose. Wasn't that how it always looked on television?

Her gaze drifted across the stubble covering his jaw, lingered on the dark smudge across his cheek. No, not a smudge. A bruise, black and purple and swollen, so dark against the pale, drawn skin of his face.

And then her gaze met his and Beth forgot to breathe. His eyes, normally such a deep, dark blue, were glazed with pain, the skin underneath them sunken and bruised. He looked...vulnerable. Weak. Not quite frail, but no longer filled with the vitality she had noticed the first time they met.

A tremor went through her, chilling her. She pulled her gaze away from his, glanced at the curious faces watching her, looked back at Adam.

"I—I just—" She tried to get the words out but couldn't, they were lodged in her throat, cutting off the air to her lungs. Panic seized her and she closed her eyes, told herself she could not—*would* not—faint. Not here. She had already embarrassed herself enough just by coming here. She wouldn't make it worse by falling flat on her face.

A second went by, then another. She cleared her throat, pulled in a deep breath, and opened her eyes. Her gaze returned to Adam and she wondered what he was thinking. Was he surprised? Happy? Angry?

She couldn't tell, realized it didn't matter.

"I—I just came to drop these off—"

"That's our cue. Come on guys, time to leave." The feminine voice, tired yet filled with authority, came from the other side of Adam's bed. Beth looked over, noticed Mikey pushing herself up from a chair. Her fiancé was by her side, helping her stand as she grabbed the pair of crutches resting against the wall.

One by one, Adam's visitors filed past her, their greetings of hello and nice-to-see-you-again nearly drowned by the buzzing in her ears. She nodded, may have replied, she didn't know. The last one to leave was Mikey, hobbling on the crutches, a cast covering her foot and lower half of her leg. She stopped at the foot of Adam's bed and gave him a look Beth couldn't decipher.

"Don't be an ass."

Beth heard the whispered words, heard Adam grunt in response. Then Mikey was hobbling past her, a small smile on her face.

"Thanks for coming."

Beth nodded, not sure what to say, not sure she'd be able to get the words out even if she did.

And then she was alone in the room, standing there with the stupid bear and balloon in her hand as Adam stared at her.

"Beth."

Chapter Twenty

Beth.

It wasn't a drug-induced hallucination, no matter what he had thought when he first saw her standing there. Adam wasn't sure if he was happy to see her, or angry at Mikey for meddling. He should have known she'd try to do something, especially after her stupid fucking comment yesterday. Damn her—

Except he couldn't work up any anger, not really. Maybe it was just a side-effect of the pain medicine, part of the soft cloud of mellowness that wrapped around him, insulating him.

Or maybe it was because the sight of Beth standing there, looking so uncertain yet so worried, stirred something deep inside him, something he hadn't felt in a long time. Something so different from the dull pain that had been hovering at the edges of awareness ever since he woke up yesterday.

Even before then.

He should say something, he knew that. But no words came to mind, nothing adequate. So he just lay there, watching her, his gaze drinking in the sight of her. She shifted, her gaze pulling away from his and darting around the room. She took a step forward, stopped, pulled her lower lip between her teeth then let out a shaky breath.

"I—I just wanted to drop these off."

His gaze dropped to the stuffed bear in her hand, with its fuzzy arms and feet poking out from the shiny black coat and pants. Adam's mouth twitched in a quick smile when he realized the little bear was a firefighter bear and that the outfit it was wearing was supposed to be turnout gear.

Beth moved forward, her steps quick, the sound of her heels clicking across the tile floor as she approached the bed. She placed the bear and the attached balloon on the rolling table at the foot of the bed and stepped back, one hand curled tightly around the strap of the purse hanging from her shoulder. She glanced at him, quickly looked away, and stepped back.

"I should probably go. You probably—"

"Stay." The word sounded desperate, almost like he was begging. Adam cleared his throat and tried to smile. "It's not exactly a quick trip back home, is it?"

"Oh. Um, no. It isn't."

Adam moved his left arm, pointed to the chair Mikey had occupied minutes earlier—the only chair in the room. "You can sit if you want. Might be more comfortable."

"You look tired. I don't want to bother you—"

"I'm fine."

She didn't look like she believed him. In fact, she looked like she was scrambling for an excuse—any excuse—to leave. If Adam was smart, he'd let her. Just thank her for the small gift and for stopping by then pretend to drift off. It would be easy enough—the drifting off part. The least little bit of activity or excitement was enough to exhaust him.

But he didn't want her to leave. He refused to examine why, didn't really care *why*. He just knew he wanted her to stay, at least for a little bit.

She hesitated long enough that Adam was sure she'd turn around and leave anyway. He didn't question the disappointment that washed over him—he'd figure it out later, when his brain wasn't quite so fuzzy with medicine and pain.

But instead of leaving, Beth slowly walked around the side of the bed and lowered herself into the chair. She placed her purse on her lap and held onto it with both hands, her grip so tight that her knuckles turned white. He saw her gaze skim along the hospital bed, quickly pass by the collection bag hanging from the side, move up to his bared stomach and chest. Her eyes finally met his. Wide, filled with emotion he couldn't read.

Silence settled between them, thick and heavy. A little awkward. Slightly uncomfortable. Adam wracked his brain, searching for something to say, anything to dispel the growing silence.

Beth cleared her throat, glanced over at him, looked away again. "Does it hurt? Never mind. I'm sorry, I shouldn't have asked, of course it hurts."

"A little, yeah." He gave her a quick smile, worried that it looked more like a grimace. He nodded toward the table where she had placed the bear. "Would you mind handing me that cup?"

She jumped from the chair so quickly, Adam was surprised it didn't tip backward. Then she was standing next to him, holding the cup in one hand, steadying the bent straw with the other. He almost told her he could hold the cup himself, that he wasn't totally helpless—but he didn't. He simply tilted his head forward and closed his lips around the straw to take a small sip of water. Beth pulled the cup away when he was finished and placed it back on the table then stood there, looking everywhere except at him.

No, that wasn't quite true. Her gaze skimmed his body, resting on each bandage, each tube, each bruise. Moisture welled in her eyes. She blinked and turned away, taking in a shaky breath.

His gut twisted, filling with knots as his heart slammed into his chest. What the hell was that about? She wasn't crying for him—she'd probably do the same for anyone else she knew. He shouldn't read anything into it.

That didn't stop the warmth spreading throughout him.

"You, uh, you look good."

Her head spun around, her brows lowered over those beautiful green-and-gold eyes. She glanced down at her outfit—black pants, black sweater—then looked back at him and shook her head. "I came right from work. I mean I—I don't usually wear all black. I wouldn't normally wear all black to a hospital. I didn't—"

"You still look good." He raised his hand, let it drop back to the mattress before he could do something stupid, like reach for her. "Especially compared to me, right?"

Her eyes rounded in surprise and her mouth parted on a choked gasp. Had he surprised her? He wasn't sure why—it was nothing more than the truth.

"I didn't mean—"

"Beth, I was joking. Or trying to. It's okay, I have a pretty good idea how I look."

She nodded, her hands gripping the railing that kept him from getting out of bed. Stupid—it wasn't like he was going anywhere anyway, not anytime soon.

He noticed her staring at his chest. No, not his chest—at the sling holding his arm in place, at the tube poking out from his side.

"Chest tube."

Beth's eyes darted to his and a faint blush covered her cheeks. "I didn't mean to stare. I'm sorry—"

"Don't be." Adam lifted his hand again, let it fold over hers. She jumped, looked down. Adam didn't move, barely breathed as he waited. Would she move away? Leave? Say anything?

Seconds stretched into a minute, each one counted out by the beating of his heart. Beth's hand relaxed under his, her fingers slowly uncurling from the railing—

Then gently threading with his.

Adam breathed a sigh of relief then started coughing. Pain exploded in his chest, sent stars shooting in front of his eyes. He felt Beth tense, sensed her panic as she called his name. He tightened his hold on her hand, tried to shake his head and tell her he was fine. Several more coughs, not as deep, then he could finally breathe. He twisted his head, pulled in several shorts breaths of oxygen flowing from the mask resting next to him. "Fuck that hurt."

"Are you okay? Should I get someone? Do you need—"

Adam silenced her panicked words by gently squeezing her hand. "No, I'm fine. They say coughing helps. The ribs hurt like a bitch, though."

"What—what happened?" The question was soft, hesitant, almost like she was afraid to ask. He saw the concern in her eyes, and the worry, so he tried to give her a reassuring smile.

"We decided to take a shortcut to the second floor."

"A shortcut?"

"Yeah. The floor gave way under us."

"OhmyGod." Beth clamped her free hand over her mouth, her eyes filling with horror. Adam immediately regretted telling her. He should have lied, should have made up some story.

"It's not that bad."

"But you could have died!"

"It's going to take a lot more than that to get rid of me." And shit, she wasn't smiling, didn't understand that he was joking. She tried to pull away but Adam tightened his hold on her hand, keeping her in place. "Beth, I was only joking. It's not as bad as it looks. Honest."

"How can you joke about something like that? Look at you! You could have been hurt even worse. You could have died. I don't—"

"Would you have missed me?" And fuck, where the hell had that stupid question come from? Why the hell had he even asked her that? It was the medication, it had to be.

And now that he asked, he was afraid of the answer. He didn't want her to say no, didn't want to hear her tell him that she wouldn't have missed him at all. But was that how she would answer? She was here, after all. She wouldn't be here if she didn't care. Right?

He waited for the space of several heartbeats, long enough to let her answer if she really wanted to. There was only silence. Adam swallowed back the unwelcome disappointment and gave her a quick smile. "I was only joking—"

"Yes." Her voice was nothing more than a hoarse whisper. She cleared her throat, her gaze focused on their clasped hands. "Yes, I would have missed you."

His heart slammed into his chest once more. He knew he needed to say something, knew he needed to respond somehow, but his mind was completely, thoroughly blank. And shit, he could feel her arm tensing, could feel her entire body tensing, knew he had only seconds before she pulled away. So he did the only thing he could think of—he tugged, hoping to pull her closer, hoping to get her to lean down for a kiss. She moved toward him, uncertainty in her gaze as he pulled her closer.

"I don't think—"

"Shh."

He tugged again and she leaned even closer, her mouth finally pressing against his. And God, she tasted so sweet, a balm to every ache and pain throbbing along his battered body.

He swept his tongue across her lips, sighed when her mouth opened for him. He ran his hand along her arm, cradled the back of her head and held her even closer. Tasting her, drinking her in.

She pulled away with a soft gasp, her wide eyes steady on his. He ran his hand through her hair, curled the pale ends around his fingers. Soft, so soft and silky.

He released her hair, ran the tip of one finger along her jaw and across her trembling lower lip before letting his hand drop back to the mattress.

"Thank you."

Confusion flashed across her face. Sculpted brows

lowered over her eyes as she tilted her head, studying him. "For what?"

"For the kiss. For coming here. For caring."

"Adam, I—"

A nurse sauntered in with a metal tray, interrupting whatever Beth had been about to say. "How's the pain, Mr. Price?"

Adam kept his gaze on Beth as he answered. "Better."

The nurse stepped around Beth, barely sparing her a glance as she reached for the IV line and injected something into it. Fuck, he should have stopped her, should have told her he wasn't ready for it. He didn't want to slide back into the fuzzy grayness, not just yet, not while Beth was still here.

The nurse was talking about X-rays, saying something about removing the chest tube tomorrow. Adam didn't pay attention, he was totally focused on Beth. He reached for her hand again, curled his fingers around it, fought against the strong pull of the medicine.

"I should leave now—"

"Stay. Please." His lids drifted shut. He groaned, fought to open them, blinked and tried to focus on Beth. "For a little bit."

"Okay. I—I'll stay. Just for a while."

A ghost of a smile played around his lips. He squeezed her hand, trying to tell her thanks, trying to tell her how much that meant to him.

How much she meant to him.

Mumbled words fell from his lips, hurried and incoherent as the grayness finally washed over him, pulling him under.

Chapter Twenty-One

Beth pulled her knees tighter against her chest, curling even deeper into the corner of the sofa. The apartment was getting darker, the light coming through the two small windows in the living room fading as night closed in. It didn't matter. Maybe the darkness would help, maybe it would swallow her whole and she wouldn't have to worry about anything.

She didn't know what to do.

She didn't know what she *wanted* to do.

And that wasn't like her.

How had it gone all wrong? How had it had happened? It was just supposed to be sex. That was it.

She should have known better. Should have known that she couldn't just have sex without getting attached. That was her problem, it always had been. She liked sex—like, *really* liked it. But she'd never been one of those women who could just hop into bed and right back out without feeling…something.

God, how could she be so stupid? She should have walked out of the bar as soon as she saw Adam that very first night, should have known he was the kind of guy who'd end up hurting her. Not because of anything he'd done—no, he'd been a perfect gentleman...

Well okay, maybe not a *gentleman*, not in the old sense of the word. She didn't think gentlemen were quite so inclined to do the things Adam had done with her. But he was *nice*. Considerate. Funny. Everything her ex wasn't.

And now she had fallen for him.

It wouldn't have been so bad, even after that last time in the parking lot. She'd known then it was too late, that she'd already fallen for him. She liked him— a *lot*. Had wondered what it would be like to actually, maybe, have a relationship with him. Yes, she knew it would never happen. Had told herself it didn't matter. She could imagine, right? Nothing wrong with that.

And that had been exactly what she'd prepared herself to do, after their last time together. No, it hadn't been easy, but since when had she ever done anything the easy way? She'd get over him, move on, get back to life as she knew it.

Until she went to see him in the hospital.

She took a deep breath and wiped her face against her shoulder. Seeing him had been a big mistake. He'd looked so...so *vulnerable*. Trying to hide the pain even though she could see it in his eyes. And that had scared her, more than anything. The idea that someone so strong, so vital, so alive, had come so close to losing it. To...to *dying*.

She couldn't imagine a world—any world— without Adam in it. That more than anything let her know she was in trouble, that she was in over her head. And when he'd held her hand and asked her to stay...

Her heart had leaped for joy, despite her mind

telling her not to read into it. He was in pain, on medicine that probably stopped him from thinking clearly. It didn't matter, though, because he'd asked her to stay. Her mind had already been made up, she'd made the decision to stay as soon as the words left his mouth, knowing she was putting her heart on the line.

What was one more time? She'd survive. She always did.

Until he uttered those last three words just before falling into whatever oblivion the medicine created for him.

I need you.

Need.

Beth had never been needed by anyone in her life. To think that someone like Adam, so strong and vital, might actually *need* her? No, it was ridiculous. Insane. Unbelievable.

It scared her to death.

It was the pain medicine talking. It had to be. No way did Adam need her. They didn't *know* each other. They had shared sex, nothing more.

Except now she was wondering if she was wrong about even that. And how stupid—how *dangerous*—was that?

So she'd left, practically running from the hospital room soon after he fell asleep. The drive back home had been a blur, a race to reclaim her sanity as she put distance between them.

Beth was fairly sure she lost that race.

If she could talk to someone, have someone tell her that she was only imagining things, that she was a fool for thinking anything could happen between them, she'd do a better job of getting these stupid fantasies out of her head. She needed a cold dose of reality to snap her out of it.

But there wasn't anyone to talk to, nobody who would really understand. Courtney would, but Courtney was dealing with her own issues. Noah's father was back in the picture. From what Courtney told her, he was trying for a reconciliation, wanted to get back together. Courtney was fighting it, afraid of getting hurt again.

Beth knew exactly how she felt.

So no, she didn't really have anyone to talk to. Who else would even possibly understand? How could she explain that she'd fallen for some guy she'd met for the sole purpose of having sex? It sounded laughingly stupid even to her own ears.

And now she was afraid she was going to make an even bigger mistake.

Beth grabbed her phone and tapped the screen, pulling up the text messages she'd received.

Adam was improving.

Adam was being released from the hospital.

Adam was going home tomorrow.

Adam needed her.

Beth closed her eyes and wondered again why the woman, Mikey, kept texting her. She didn't know Beth, didn't know anything about her. Didn't know that she was nothing more than a casual hook-up for Adam.

Her mistake had been in telling Mikey that—because apparently Mikey *did* know. At least enough. And oh God, how embarrassing was that? It didn't matter that Mikey told her she was the only woman Adam had ever introduced to his shift. So what? It meant nothing.

Except Mikey was convinced it did.

Mikey was convinced Beth was exactly what

Adam needed.

No. Absolutely not. Beth couldn't allow herself to think that, not even in the middle of the night, in the deepest, most secret places of her mind that came alive during her dreams. To believe that, even for a second, would prove fatal.

Beth had experienced heartache before, but she always survived. She knew now it was because none of the relationships had the power to really hurt her—because she hadn't given them the power. Hadn't really given them that much of herself, had always held something back.

It was different with Adam, and she wasn't sure why. Somehow, somewhere along the way, she'd given him...well, maybe not *power*. But she'd given him a piece of herself that she'd never given to anyone else. She didn't know how, didn't know why, only knew that it was too late to take it back.

That didn't mean she intended to deliberately set herself up for heartache. She could still save herself from that, all she had to do was distance herself. Not think about him, not let those stupid fantasies play out in her mind.

Except Mikey didn't want to let her do that.

Beth had asked her why. Why was she so determined? Why was she suddenly so involved?

The answer had brought tears to Beth's eyes, had shattered the protective wall she'd tried so hard to keep in place.

He saved my life.

And that's when Beth learned exactly what had happened the night Adam got hurt. The fire, the explosion, the floor collapse. How he'd grabbed Mikey and protected her with his own body, how he'd risked himself to protect her—and her unborn child.

"Oh, damn. Damn, damn, damn." Beth tossed the phone to the side and wiped her eyes. It shouldn't matter, none of it. She needed to protect herself. She needed to *not* be stupid, for once in her life.

She needed to walk away, put it all behind her. To save herself before she made a huge mistake.

The phone vibrated. Once, twice, three times. Beth stared at it, afraid to pick it up, afraid of what she'd see.

Afraid of what she'd do.

But she reached for it anyway, read the text messages flashing across the screen.

And knew she was going to make the biggest mistake of her life.

Chapter Twenty-Two

Sweat beaded on his forehead, his breath coming in short gasps by the time he reached the second-floor landing of the apartment building. Adam leaned against the wall, trying to catch his breath as Jimmy stepped around him to open the door. Fuck, it felt like he'd just run a marathon instead of walking up one flight of steps.

Jimmy looked at him over his shoulder as he held the door open. "You okay over there?"

"Would you do anything if I wasn't?"

"Hey, you're the one who said you didn't help, who insisted you could do everything on your own."

Adam grunted, considered telling him to fuck off, changed his mind. He didn't have the energy. Besides, cussing Jimmy out would be nothing more than wasted breath because the man wouldn't care.

Adam pushed off the wall and walked the few steps into his apartment. The air wasn't as stale as he expected, probably because Mikey and Angie had been there yesterday to clean up. Not that there was much to clean up—Adam had never been a slob to begin with. But when an apartment sat empty for eight days, there was bound to be a little dust.

Eight days. Christ, he still couldn't believe it. It had seemed so much longer, the days blurring into each other, marked by nothing more than varying degrees of pain. They had finally sent him home today, with a long list of instructions, precautions, and prescriptions.

Jimmy moved into the kitchen and rummaged through the pharmacy bag, pulling out different bottles of pills and lining them up along the counter. He held one up, studied the label, then grabbed a glass from the cabinet and filled it with water.

"It's time for this one. You need to take another dose before you go to bed tonight. You about ready for a pain pill? It looks like you could use one."

Adam shook his head. "No, not yet."

"You sure? You don't want to wait until the pain gets so bad it's unbearable. You're supposed to stay ahead of it."

"Yeah, I know. And yeah, I'm sure." He moved to the counter and lowered himself onto one of the stools as Jimmy slid the glass toward him. Adam tossed the pill into his mouth and washed it down with a long gulp of water, then winced when pain shot through his shoulder from moving the wrong way.

"You sure about that pill?"

"Yeah, I'm sure. The only thing I want right now is a long hot shower. I haven't felt clean since that fucking fire."

"I still don't think that's a good idea, not with that fracture."

"The doc said I could, so that's exactly what I'm going to do. Trust me, I don't plan on moving my arm any more than I have to."

"Still don't know why I got suckered into helping you out today. The last thing I want to do is help you wash your sorry ass."

"Then don't. I can manage myself."

Jimmy laughed, the sound a short burst of disbelief. So okay, maybe Adam did need some help. They both knew it. That didn't mean he had to be excited about it.

"Well, whenever you're ready."

"Yeah, give me a minute." Adam closed his eyes and slowly straightened, doing his best not to jostle the arm. It felt good just to be home. To sit on his own furniture, even if it was just a stool. To breathe in the scents of home instead of the sharp odors of disinfectant.

He breathed in again, frowning, then shook his head as recognition dawned. Cinnamon and pine, just in time for the upcoming holiday season that was right around the corner. They'd obviously used scented air freshener or something when they came over yesterday.

It actually wasn't that bad. Maybe he'd ask Mikey what kind, just in case he wanted to use some again. Just in case he had company or something.

Yeah, that probably wasn't going to happen, not unless it was the guys from work. Why the hell would he waste air freshener on any of them?

Adam slid off the stool, his steps slow and cautious as he made his way back to his room. Jimmy followed, turning into the bathroom. He heard the sound of the faucet being turned on, heard the sound of water running. Christ, this was a new low, needing help to take a fucking shower.

Whatever. He didn't care. As long as he could get clean.

He turned on the light in his bedroom then came to a stop in the doorway. What the fuck? Damn Mikey. Why the hell had she brought that stupid fucking thing here? He'd told her he didn't want it, told her to take it home or give it away or toss it out.

Did she really think bringing the stupid stuffed bear here and leaving it on his pillow was going to make any difference? No, it wasn't.

There was nothing between Beth and him, no matter how much Mikey insisted otherwise. Yes, Beth had stopped by to visit. Yes, he liked her. Okay, yeah, maybe he even cared about her—for as much as he was capable of caring about anyone. But he hadn't heard from Beth since the day she had come to see him, the day she had given him that stupid—that cute—little fireman bear.

Adam was pretty sure he knew why he hadn't heard from her. It was because of whatever he'd said just before he totally crashed under the pain medication. The problem was, he had no idea what he said.

No, the real problem was—he thought he *did* know. Maybe.

And what the hell. It didn't matter. Beth had been gone when he came to. Which was fine. She deserved better anyway.

A hell of a lot better than what he could ever give her.

"Are you jumping in here or did you pass out on the floor?" Jimmy's voice floated in from the bathroom. Adam stepped toward the dresser, pointedly ignoring the bear resting against his pillow, and grabbed everything he needed: socks, underwear, sweatpants, t-shirt. He glanced down at the t-shirt, frowned, then placed it back in the drawer. No way in hell would he be able to get a t-shirt on, not yet.

He hobbled back to the bathroom and placed the clean clothes on the small shelf unit tucked into the corner. Then it was time to strip down, something easier said than done in spite of the loose clothes he was wearing.

Jimmy grumbled, muttering under his breath the entire time he helped. Adam almost told him to leave, that he'd do it himself—except he couldn't, and they both knew it.

"I don't know why the hell you just can't wait to have your girlfriend come help you out."

"I don't have a girlfriend."

"Yeah, right. That's why she came to see you."

"One time. Doesn't mean anything."

"If you say so. That's why—"

"Fuck. Holy shit. Watch it. That fucking hurt." Adam grabbed his right shoulder, his eyes closed against the hard throbbing caused by Jimmy pulling the sling free.

"Sorry, accident."

"Yeah, I bet."

Jimmy ignored the accusation then slid the shower curtain to the side. "You sure you can handle this by yourself? You don't want to wait?"

"Yeah, I'm sure." Adam climbed over the edge of the tub, each movement slow and careful so he wouldn't jostle his arm or shoulder or ribs. Although the ribs didn't hurt too much, as long as he was careful.

He closed his eyes and stood under the hot spray of water, his body slowly relaxing as warmth seeped into him. God, this was almost like heaven.

No, heaven would be if Beth was here with him.

He stifled a groan when he noticed the first faint stirrings in his cock. Great, just what didn't need. He pushed all thoughts of Beth from his mind and reached for the shower gel, squeezing some onto the top of his head, some more onto his chest.

Lathering up using his left hand was awkward, clumsy. More than once he had started to use his right, only to be stopped by a quick stab of pain. It wasn't the most thorough cleansing he'd ever done, but he still felt a hell of a lot better than he had earlier.

Adam waited until the water changed from hot to lukewarm then reached behind him to turn it off. He wiped the water from his face then stuck his hand outside the shower curtain.

"Jimmy, can you hand me a towel?"

Silence.

Adam sighed, waved his hand around, blindly searching for the towel rack. "Jimmy!"

The towel was thrust into his hand without a word. Adam muttered his impatient thanks then wiped down as best he could before rubbing the towel over his head. He draped it over his shoulder then pushed back the shower curtain, ready to step out.

And froze.

He squeezed his eyes shut, wondering if maybe he fell in the shower. Wondering if he hit his head and was suffering from some kind of weird hallucination.

He opened his eyes and stared.

No, he wasn't imagining things. Beth was standing in the doorway of the bathroom, her hands clasped tightly in front of her, looking as uncomfortable as he felt. Her gaze dropped, shot back to his face as a blush spread across her face.

Adam scrambled for the towel, tried to untangle it and get it spread in front of him. It dropped into the tub, completely useless. He started to bend down to grab it, felt a sharp pain and quickly straightened.

"Uh. I—Beth."

"Hi."

"Uh, yeah. Hi." Adam climbed over the edge of the tub, grabbed another towel from the towel rack and awkwardly wrapped it around his waist. "What—what are you doing here?"

Shit, did he have to sound so unwelcoming? So stunned? Yes, he was surprised—totally blown away. But it was a good surprise—he thought. Maybe. Unless he really had knocked himself unconscious and was only imagining her standing there.

She rocked back on her heels, her gaze dancing around the small room before finally resting on him again. "Someone said you, uh, might need a haircut."

"A haircut?"

"Yeah. To fix, you know, the singed ends."

Adam almost raised his hand to run it through his hair, caught himself—and the towel—at the last minute. "A haircut?"

Beth fidgeted, uncertainty clear in her gaze. She looked away, staring down at her feet. "I can come back—"

"No!" Adam took a step toward her, stopped, cleared his throat. "No. I mean, you're here, right? Might as well."

"Good. Okay. Good. I'll meet you in the dining room."

Adam nodded, his mind still reeling. "Is, uh, is Jimmy still here?"

"No, he left already. Why? Do you need help?"

Fuck. He wished he could say no. He really wanted to say no. But no way in hell could he manage the sling and the pants by himself, not using his left hand. Not without hurting himself.

He swallowed back his pride and offered a small grin. "Yeah. Probably. I mean, at least with the sling."

Beth didn't hesitate. She grabbed the sling from the counter and closed the distance between them. She unfolded it, studying it with a frown before tossing him a confused look. Adam told her how to place it, turned around so she could settle it over his head. Her fingers brushed the back of his neck, grazed the skin of his left shoulder. He heard her gasp, felt her fingers trace the bruise that ran along his back. Gentle, featherlight, as if she was afraid of hurting him.

Adam closed his eyes and held his breath, told his body not to react, told himself her touch meant nothing. Even if it did, there was nothing he could do about it, not now.

"It's from the bottle. Where I landed on it. It doesn't really hurt."

"It looks like it would." Her fingers hesitated, so warm against his skin, then finally moved away. Her movements turned brisk, quick and efficient as she fastened the sling around him and secured it in place. "Anything else?"

Shit. Could he manage the sweatpants with one hand? Maybe now that his arm was immobilized, it wouldn't jostle so much. He'd still have to bend over, still have to struggle to get his legs through each opening.

He had to do it himself. He couldn't let Beth help him, not when his cock was—not surprisingly—

already coming to life. Yeah, she'd seen it before. Held it, stroked it, sucked it. But this…this was different. Too intimate somehow. Too personal. It made him feel vulnerable, required a trust he wasn't quite ready to give.

A trust he wasn't sure he'd ever be able to give. Not just to Beth—to anyone.

"No, I think I'm good."

He sensed her disappointment, heard the hesitation in her voice when she spoke. "You're sure?"

"Yeah. Yeah, I'm good. Thanks."

"I'll be in the other room if you need anything."

He heard the door close behind her, released the breath he hadn't realized he'd been holding. What the fuck was wrong with him?

Everything. Nothing.

He grabbed the sweatpants and lowered himself to the edge of the tub. Then he just stared at them, the dark blue lettering running down the left leg blurring against the gray fabric.

What the fuck was wrong with him?

The question—somehow an accusation—spun through his mind, over and over. Was he so fucked up he couldn't accept help from a woman who obviously cared about him? Was he so afraid of admitting to any vulnerability that he'd rather risk hurting himself than asking for—accepting—help?

If it had been Jimmy—or Dave or Jay or fuck, even Mikey—he would have never hesitated. But Beth? He couldn't do it. Couldn't let any weakness be exposed.

Couldn't let himself trust.

Not in himself, not in the chance that Beth really might care for him. He didn't want her to care for him, was afraid of what that might mean.

Was afraid he'd do something wrong, that he'd twist and warp whatever she felt until it became something else, something dirty and sick and depraved. Until it blackened and shriveled and died.

Just like him.

Just like his soul.

Chapter Twenty-Three

Just like his soul.

How long had Adam been sitting there, his mind fighting the truth of who he was? If he was smart, if he had any decency at all, he'd tell Beth to leave. It was for her own good. She deserved so much better than anything he could give her. He'd tried telling Mikey that, that day in the hospital. Tried telling her every single time she brought it up after that. But she wouldn't believe him, had brushed off his concerns, had told him he was being too hard on himself.

He should have told Mikey why. If she knew half of the things he'd done, she would have never called Beth. Would have never meddled and tried to play matchmaker. He should have told her.

But then Beth wouldn't be here.

And God help him, he didn't want her to leave. It was selfish of him, but he wanted her here. Wanted to know she cared for him. Wanted, if only for an hour or two, to believe that she saw something inside him, something good. Something worth caring about.

He was a fool. Such a fucking fool.

A knock sounded on the door, soft and hesitant. "You okay in there? Need any help?"

No. Tell her no. Tell her to go away, to leave. To go home and forget she ever met him.

"Adam?" She knocked again, a little louder this time.

He opened his mouth, willed the words to come out, told himself it was for the best. It would be the first selfless thing he had done in a long time. But only a harsh croak came out.

"Adam?" She repeated his name, concern heavy in her voice. He saw the handle turn, saw the door ease open, yet he still couldn't get the words out, couldn't make himself tell her what she needed to hear—the truth, of who and what he was.

Not even when she hurried toward him. Not when she kneeled down in front of him and covered his shaking hand with her own. When had he started shaking? Why?

Concern filled her eyes, along with something else, something he didn't want to see. Something he didn't deserve.

Tell her, dammit.

But he couldn't get the words out. Couldn't even form them in his mind.

What did she see when she looked at him like that? She should be able to see him for what he really was. She should be able to see the blackness of his empty soul reflected in his eyes. Why didn't she see it?

"You okay?" She didn't wait for him to answer, just took the sweatpants from his hand and shook them out. Her hand, warm and gentle, closed around one ankle and guided his foot through the leg opening.

She did the same with the other foot then tugged the pants up to his knees. Her fingers brushed against his inner thigh. She hesitated then released a small laugh, the sound quiet, almost breathless.

"This is a little weird, dressing you. All the other times, it's always been the opposite."

The sound that bubbled from Adam's throat couldn't be called a laugh. It was too harsh, too strangled. Filled with self-deprecation. "I'm an ass."

"Why? Because you need help? Don't be stupid."

"No, that's not why."

Beth pushed to her feet. He expected her to ask why but she didn't. Instead, she leaned down and held her arm out in front of him. "Here, take my arm, I'll help you up."

Adam looked up at her. "Why?"

"So you don't hurt yourself—"

"No. Why are you here? Why? I don't understand."

She was quiet for so long, her gaze steady on his as she watched him. A small smile, tinged with a hint of sadness, flashed across her face as she shrugged. "I don't know why. I just know—"

She hesitated, chewed on her lower lip for a second then shrugged again. "I just—I guess I feel like I need to be here. I know it doesn't make sense. I can't explain it. Now come on, take my arm and I'll help you up."

Adam hesitated, wanting to ask her to explain anyway. To make him understand. But he was afraid to, afraid of pushing, afraid of any answer she might give him. So he reached for her arm, let her ease him to a standing position as he pushed up with his legs. Beth leaned down and grabbed the waistband of the sweatpants, quickly tugged them up over his thighs and hips then took the towel from him and slung it over her shoulder.

"Everything's set up in the dining room. This won't take long, then you can eat. And then you should probably lay down. You shouldn't overdo anything the first day home."

Adam followed her out to the dining room, let her help him into one of the chairs. She draped a plastic cape around his shoulders, settled another one on the floor, then reached in front of him for a comb and a pair of scissors.

She ran her fingers through his hair, straightening the damp strands, using the comb here and there. He felt her pull a section straight, heard the faint clipping of the scissors as she trimmed the ends. "This really isn't bad at all. You won't even see a real difference once I'm done."

"You should leave."

She paused, the scissors going still. Adam heard her take a deep breath, imagined he could feel the warmth of it as she exhaled. "Wow. A few snips and already you're lodging a complaint. Usually my customers are pretty happy when I'm done."

"Beth, it's not—that's not what I meant." He started to turn his head but she held it still with the heel of one hand. She ran the comb through his hair, made a few snips with the scissors, combed another section.

Snip, snip.

"Then what do you mean?"

"I—" He hesitated, not sure what to say.

Tell her.

He needed to tell her.

"I—I'm fucked up, Beth. Really fucked up."

She paused again, her hand momentarily dropping to his left shoulder. And God, her touch felt so good, so comforting. He wanted to reach up and grab her hand, to hold onto it and never let go. He curled his fingers into a fist and forced his hand to stay in his lap.

"Is it your shoulder? Is it worse—"

"No. No, it's not that. Nothing like that." He pulled in a deep breath, winced at the pain and quickly released it, took a shorter one. "It's—it's me. I—the things I do. That I've done."

Beth moved her hand. She was going to leave now, he knew it. It was for the best, she deserved so much better.

But she didn't leave. She ran her fingers through his hair again, resumed cutting with the scissors.

Snip. Snip.

"What kind of things?"

And fuck, he couldn't tell her. He didn't want to tell her. But she deserved to know. *Needed* to know.

He closed his eyes, struggled to find the right words.

And then he told her. Everything. How he'd walked in on his girlfriend. What he saw. What he did. How he felt after. How he'd discovered the chatroom. The hook-ups, the casual encounters. Every single detail, all of it. The words fell from his mouth as if something had burst inside him, until there was nothing left to tell.

Until he felt…empty. Hollow.

Beth never said a word the entire time, just kept standing behind him, running her fingers through his hair and cutting. She finally stopped, placed the scissors and comb back on the table, and carefully removed the cape. He wanted to turn around and look at her, needed to see the disgust and loathing on her face.

Needed her to tell him what kind of sick and depraved monster he really was.

But she didn't say anything, just quietly gathered the plastic sheet from the floor and carefully folded it before carrying it into the kitchen. He watched her throw it into the trash can, turned away when she walked back into the dining room.

He had lied to himself—he didn't want to see her face. Couldn't bear to see the disgust in her eyes when she looked at him. It didn't matter. She'd leave now, just walk out and that would be that.

Except she didn't. She pulled out the chair to his left and took a seat, carefully folded her hands in front of her and rested them on the table, then let out a shaky breath.

It was the only sound in the apartment for a long time. Almost too long.

"So you think you're twisted and warp because you've met women in a chatroom for sex?"

"Yes. Didn't you hear what I said? The things I've done? It wasn't just the sex. It was—"

"We met in the chatroom. Does that mean I'm twisted and warped?"

Adam flinched as if he'd been hit in the chest. Is that what she thought he was saying? Did she really think he thought of her as twisted and warped?

"No. God no. Not even close. That's not what I meant, Beth. You're not—"

"Then why are *you*?"

"Didn't you hear what I said? All the things I've done?"

"What about the things *we've* done?"

"That's not what I'm talking about. I'm talking about—"

"Did you ever force anyone?"

"What? No! I would never—"

"So it was all consensual?"

"Of course. That doesn't mean—"

"Were any of the women underage?"

"Hell no! Absolutely not. I would never—"

"Then why do you think you're twisted and warped? Why are you so convinced of that?"

"Didn't you hear me?" He pushed away from the table, got to his feet and started pacing in an angry circle. "I walked in on my girlfriend fucking another guy and got a fucking hard on! I *joined in*. How is that not fucked up? I've had a threesome, got off watching two girls fuck each other. How is that not fucked up? It is. *I* am. Just...I'm just fucked up, period."

"I've, uh, I've never had a threesome but don't most guys get excited about watching two girls?"

"Beth—"

"Don't they? That's what I've always heard. My, uh, my ex-boyfriend used to watch porn all the time. That was what turned him on. The girls, I mean. He would get angry because I wouldn't—I never—"

"Fuck." Adam ran his hand over his face, his gut clenching at the pain and humiliation on Beth's face. He moved closer to her, kneeled down next to her and reached for her hand. "Your ex was a fucking asshole then."

"But you did it—"

"Yeah. Once. It wasn't my thing." And how the hell had the conversation taken this turn? Why couldn't she see how twisted he was? Why was she still sitting there, her fingers clutching his, instead of running out the door?

"Beth—"

"He's why I went to the chatroom, you know."

"What?"

"He used to tell me that—that I wasn't...you know. So I wanted to prove I was."

Anger seared his veins, burning and intense. His hand tightened around hers, tugged until she looked over at him. "Then he really is an asshole who doesn't know what he's talking about. Beth, you're one of the most sensual, giving women I've ever met. And you deserve so much more."

Couldn't she see that? Didn't she know? Her ex certainly didn't deserve her.

And neither did he.

He pulled her hand from his and sat back down, suddenly weary. Empty. It had been a long day, he was tired and drained. That had to be why he felt the way he did, so...out of sorts. Confused. He must not have explained things the right way. If he had, Beth wouldn't still be sitting here.

"Can I ask you a question?"

Adam looked over, saw the hesitancy in her eyes, the slight blush coloring her cheeks.

"What?"

"It's—it's personal."

Adam laughed, the sound flat and hollow. She was worried about asking something personal? After everything he'd just told her? "Sure. Okay. What?"

"When...when you were with your girlfriend, did you see anyone else?"

"You mean, did I sleep around on her? No. Not on her, not on anyone else I dated. I don't go for that shit."

"How about—I mean, I know we weren't dating but—never mind. Forget I asked." She looked away, the blush on her cheeks turning an even deeper shade of red.

"I haven't been with anyone else since the night I met you, Beth."

Her head spun around, her eyes widening in surprise. She shook her head, gave him a brief smile. "It's okay if you have. I understand. You don't have to say that just to make me feel better.

"I'm not saying it to make you feel better—I'm saying it because it's the truth. I might be a lot of things, but I'm not a liar."

Something flared in the depths of her eyes, something he couldn't decipher. Gratitude? Hell, he didn't want her gratitude. He wanted—

Fuck. No. No, he couldn't go there. Not after everything he just told her, not when he knew she'd eventually come to her senses and walk out.

It didn't matter. It didn't change how he felt. He wanted *her*. He wanted Beth. He didn't know what he was feeling, was afraid to put a name to it, afraid to look too closely at it. All he knew was that he wanted Beth.

And he didn't deserve her.

She leaned forward, concern etched on her face as she grabbed his hand. "Are you okay? You look—is it your shoulder? Your chest?"

"Uh, yeah. Yeah, I guess. My chest."

"Do you want a pill? I'll get it for you—"

"No. No, I think I just need to lie down for a little bit. That's all." He pushed out of the chair, surprised when Beth stood up with him. She stayed right beside him as he walked down the hall, his steps heavy, shuffling. He kept expecting her to leave, to turn around and say goodnight.

To say goodbye.

She followed him into his room instead, hurried to the bed and pulled down the comforter and blanket and top sheet. She hesitated, studying the stuffed bear for a few seconds before moving it to the nightstand. Then she was back by his side, her hand steady on his arm as he climbed the two steps into the bed and stretched out.

"Do you need the pillows adjusted at all? Maybe one by your right side?"

"No, this is good for right now."

"Are you sure? If you need anything, just let me know."

If he needed anything.

Adam hesitated, called himself a fool for even thinking of asking. He shouldn't, had no right—

But he asked anyway.

"Actually, there is something you could do. If you want to, I mean. If not, I understand. You're probably—"

"What?"

Adam swallowed, wondered how big a mistake he was making. Fuck, it wasn't like he could embarrass himself even more by asking, right?

"Would you mind laying down with me? Just for a little bit?"

He expected her to say no. He didn't expect the soft smile that curled her full lips, or the flash of something bright that shone in her eyes. She nodded and climbed up into the bed, stretched out along his left side and settled the blanket over them.

"Is this okay?"

Adam tightened his arm around her and pressed a kiss to her forehead.
"Yeah. Perfect."

Chapter Twenty-Four

Warmth surrounded her, a cocoon of protection. Soothing, comforting. She snuggled deeper, reveling in how natural it felt. How right.

How *perfect*.

Beth's lids fluttered open as the dream faded away. Only the warmth was still there, that feeling of being protected. Wanted. Needed.

Cherished.

She blinked, jerked back when she saw the deep blue eyes staring at her. So deep, she could drown in their depths. Her heart slammed into her chest and her breath caught in her lungs. She must still be dreaming, must still be floating in that fantasy world that had pulled her so completely under and held her under its spell.

"Hey."

Adam's voice, thick with sleep. His smile, full and sensual.

It wasn't a dream. She was here, with Adam. In his bed.

And he was watching her with so much...*tenderness*. No, she must be dreaming. Why else would she be seeing that tenderness in his eyes when he looked at her? She pushed up on one elbow, realized she had been using his chest as a pillow. Her gaze caught on the sling and guilt swept through her. Oh God, had she hurt him? Made his injury worse? He didn't look like he was in pain but that didn't mean—

She ran a shaking hand through her hair and looked around, the room slowly coming into focus as the final wisps of sleep faded away. They were in his room, in his giant bed designed for decadence. Oh God, she had fallen asleep in his arms. She hadn't meant to, hadn't planned—

She cleared her throat and looked over at him, embarrassment flooding her cheeks when she realized he was still watching her. A faint smile teased the corners of his mouth as he ran his hand along her arm. Her skin pebbled and tingled under his touch as warmth unfurled deep inside her.

She cleared her throat again and looked away, afraid of what he might see on her face, in her eyes. "I didn't mean to fall asleep—"

"I'm not complaining."

"But your shoulder—"

"I'll survive." There was something in his voice, something warm, enticing. She turned back to him, trying to figure out why he sounded so different.

Why was he watching her like that? Why was that small smile hovering on his mouth? Shouldn't he be asleep? Shouldn't he be resting, letting his body heal? She shouldn't be in bed with him, certainly shouldn't be sleeping with her head on his chest.

Beth struggled to sit up all the way, tried not to

stare at his broad chest, at the flat planes of his stomach and the thin line of hair that disappeared into the waistband of those loose sweatpants.

Heat filled her face and she looked away. "I'm sorry. I didn't mean to stay."

Adam jerked his hand from her arm. The air around them changed, grew chilled and tense. Beth frowned, turned back to face him. The smile was gone from his mouth. A muscle twitched in his clenched jaw as he watched her. His gaze was hooded now, filled with shadows she didn't understand.

Shadows that leached the warmth from her body and left her chilled and oddly empty.

"Oh." His voice was flat, emotionless. He looked away, pushed up with his good arm and swung his legs over the side of the bed so his back was to her. "You've probably got things to do."

Why did he sound so...cold? Remote?

Beth slid across the bed on her knees, her feet tangling in the silky sheets. An impatient groan of frustration escaped her as she kicked the sheets away then reached for Adam. His body tensed under her hand and for a brief second, she worried that he'd pull away. That he'd brush off her hand and slide off the edge of the bed and walk away.

"Yes, I do. I'm supposed to be fixing you something to eat. I'm supposed to be helping you—not making things worse by falling asleep on top of you."

Adam twisted to the side, his brows pulled low over his eyes. His gaze was a little chilled, a little distant, as he studied her. "You said you didn't mean to stay."

"I didn't. I was only going to lay down with you until you fell asleep."

His frown deepened. "And then what?"

"Then I was going to go back out to the living room and..." Her voice trailed off. The expression in his eyes had changed again. Not quite as distant, filled with confusion now. And something...something else.

He drew his legs back on the bed, pushing up with his heels until his back was resting against the headboard. He stretched his legs in front of him, crossed them at the ankles, then grabbed a pillow and held it against his right side. His gaze was on her the entire time. Thoughtful, intent, questioning. She scooted away, a little intimidated, not sure what was going through his mind.

"Why are you here, Beth?"

"What do you mean?"

"Why are you here? Now. With me. Why?"

"Because I—" She swallowed, willed her heart to stop its insane pounding. "Because you need help and—"

"But why you? Why not Jimmy? Or Dave? Or Dale or Jay or even Mikey? Why you?"

"Because...because Mikey thought—"

"Did she put you up to this? Talk you into coming here?"

"No! I mean, yes. Maybe. A little."

Adam's mouth hardened into a thin line, but only for a second. He breathed in, a quick inhalation through his nose, then released it slowly.

"So you're here because, for some reason I can only guess at, Mikey talked you into it?" He closed his eyes and shook his head, muttered something under his breath that she couldn't make out. "That's why you stayed, even after I told you everything I did?"

"No, of course not."

"Then why, Beth? Tell me. *Why* are you here?"

A brief flare of anger flashed inside her and she ruthlessly pushed it away. He wasn't making any sense, at least not that she could understand. But he was hurt, he probably wasn't thinking straight because of the pain and the medicine. "Because you need help."

"Not as a lame ass attempt at matchmaking or obligation, I don't."

"What?" Beth narrowed her eyes, the anger springing to life again. No, not anger. Frustration and confusion and...and—yes, a little anger.

"What?" She repeated the question, louder this time. "*Obligation?* Obligation for *what?* Do you really think I would be here if I didn't *want* to be?"

Adam's eyes grew a little wider as her voice grew louder. And was that a smile on his face? Yes. Yes, it was. He was trying to fight it, she could see that. And he was failing miserably.

"You want to be with me? After everything I told you, you still want to be with me?"

That was the last straw. Something inside her snapped. Frustration, emotion, uncertainty. All the confusion from the last four months, ever since she'd first laid eyes on the man in front of her. She grabbed one of the pillows, fisted her hands into the downy softness, then swung it against the mattress. Hard. Over and over, a different curse word escaping from between clenched teeth each time she swung.

Adam started laughing. A quiet chuckle at first, growing louder each time she swung the pillow. Beth glared at him, was tempted to hurl the pillow right at his smiling face. But she couldn't, no matter how frustrated she was, because she didn't want to hurt him.

"You're an ass!"

Adam nodded, still laughing. "I know."

"It's not funny."

"I know."

"Stop laughing!"

"Someone has a little bit of a temper."

"I do not!"

"You do. It's cute."

Beth swung the pillow one more time. He laughed harder then grabbed his side, a hiss of pain escaping his parted lips. Beth leaned forward, her anger and frustration instantly evaporating, changing into concern as she reached for him.

"Did you hurt yourself? Did you make it worse?"

Adam pressed his hand against his side and shook his head. But damn if he didn't start laughing again, just a little quieter this time. Beth narrowed her eyes and pushed away, ready to climb down from the stupid bed and storm out of the room.

Adam caught her hand, his fingers threading with hers and holding her in place.

"Don't leave."

Beth glared at him, wondered if she was faster than he was, considering he was hurt.

Probably not.

He tugged on her hand. "Come here."

"No."

He tugged again. "Come here."

"*No.*"

The laughter faded from his eyes, replaced with something dangerously warm, frighteningly intense. "Please."

And oh God, his voice. Soft, caressing. Not pleading, not really—she couldn't imagine a man like Adam ever pleading—but still somehow vulnerable. It reached out, called to her, drew her in.

Pulled her over the edge she had been trying to scramble away from for weeks now.

He tugged her closer, settled her so she was straddling his lap, then reached up with his free hand and caressed her cheek. His eyes darkened, deep pools of blue that pulled her under his spell.

"You really want to be here? With me?"

Why did he keep asking her that? Hadn't she admitted her foolish weakness already? Did he really need more?

Realization slammed into her as she looked deeper into his eyes. He *did* need more. Not because of ego, not because of conceit—but because he truly couldn't believe it.

And it suddenly made sense, everything he'd told her earlier. He'd been trying to push her away, trying to convince her to leave because he honestly didn't think he deserved any better.

"Oh, Adam." She turned her head and pressed a kiss against his palm. "Yes, I do. I—I care about you."

A spark of light flared in his eyes, chasing away the last of the shadows. He grinned, wrapped his hand around her neck, and pulled her down for a kiss. Long, deep, filled with unspoken promises.

He pulled away, his eyes searching hers. "Stay with me."

"Okay."

"I mean it."

"Okay."

"Tonight. Tomorrow. Next week. Next month. I want you to stay with me. I *need* you to stay with me."

Beth nodded, her throat too thick with emotion to say anything. This was all new—for both of them.

There were things they needed to talk about, things they both needed to figure out.

But for now—

For now, it was enough.

She nodded again, lowered her mouth to his, gave herself up to the kiss. Deep, possessing. Giving and taking. Desire and need exploded inside her and she pressed herself even closer, ran her hands through his hair as she gave herself over to him.

She eased away, finally aware of the hard thickness of his cock pressing between her legs. A frown creased her face and she looked down at him. "You can't be serious."

He smiled, the dimple showing in his cheek. "All I have to do is think about you and I get hard."

"We can't. Not right now. You'll hurt yourself."

"Maybe I can't, but *you* can."

"Adam, no. I couldn't."

But she could.

And they did.

Epilogue

One Year Later

"We're going to be late."

"No, we won't."

"The christening starts in two hours. Mikey will be furious if we're not there on time."

Beth had a point. Adam was one of the godfathers to Mikey and Nick's baby girl, a healthy happy three-month-old they had named Shannon. It went without saying that Shannon would be the most protected girl in the mid-Atlantic. How could she not be, with so many uncles?

But Adam wasn't worried about Shannon, not right now. He was completely focused on Beth. How had it happened? He hadn't planned on a relationship, had convinced himself it would never happen. He was too sick, too twisted, too depraved.

And he had certainly never expected to fall in love.

But he had. Firmly, deeply, madly in love.

Now if he could just convince Beth that they had

plenty of time.

"I love you."

She narrowed her eyes, her expression letting him know that she was well aware of what he was trying to do. "I love you, too. We still don't have time."

"Just a quickie."

Her eyebrows shot up in disbelief. "That word isn't in your vocabulary."

"There's a first time for everything."

"We're going to be late."

"We won't be late. I swear."

Beth frowned, disbelief filling her eyes. Okay, maybe he'd said similar things in the past. He always meant them. It wasn't his fault that he lost total track of all time whenever he was Beth.

Her gaze darted to the master bedroom shower, a large custom walk-in job with a tile bench and a stone floor. Steam floated from the copper shower head, forming condensation on the large glass door. Her gaze slid from the shower and danced across his naked body. Desire flared in her eyes as she watched him stroke the hard length of his cock.

Her throat worked as she swallowed. Adam held his breath, waiting to see what she would do. Beth laughed, whipped the towel from her body, and hurried into the shower.

Adam breathed a sigh of relief and hurried in after her. She spun around, her arms wrapping around his neck as his mouth closed over hers. Hot, needy, demanding. She dragged one hand along his shoulder, down across his chest, his stomach. Lower still. Breath rushed from his chest on a long moan when her hand closed around his cock, stroking him. God, her touch. He'd never get tired of it, would always hunger for it.

Just her touch was enough to bring him to the brink.

He moaned again, slid his mouth from hers, grabbed her by the hips and lifted. Legs wrapped around his waist as he braced her against the smooth wall. Her head fell back, a long moan escaping her as he drove his cock into the tight heat of her pussy.

As he drove himself home.

Finally finding himself in the woman who loved him.

###

ABOUT THE AUTHOR

Lisa B. Kamps is the author of the best-selling series *The Baltimore Banners*, featuring "hard-hitting, heart-melting hockey players" [USA Today], on and off the ice. Her *Firehouse Fourteen* series features hot and heroic firefighters who put more than their lives on the line. She's introduced a whole new team of hot hockey players who play hard and love even harder in her newest series, *The York Bombers*.

In a previous life, she worked as a firefighter with the Baltimore County Fire Department then did a very brief (and not very successful) stint at bartending in east Baltimore, and finally served as the Director of Retail Operations for a busy Civil War non-profit.

Lisa currently lives in Maryland with her husband and two sons (who are mostly sorta-kinda out of the house), one very spoiled Border Collie, two cats with major attitude, several head of cattle, and entirely too many chickens to count. When she's not busy writing or chasing animals, she's cheering loudly for her favorite hockey team, the Washington Capitals--or going through withdrawal and waiting for October to roll back around!

Interested in reaching out to Lisa? She'd love to hear from you, and there are several ways to contact her:

Website: www.LisaBKamps.com
Newsletter: www.lisabkamps.com/signup/
Email: LisaBKamps@gmail.com
Facebook Author Page:
www.facebook.com/authorLisaBKamps

Kamps Korner Facebook Group:
www.facebook.com/groups/1160217000707067/
Twitter: twitter.com/LBKamps
Goodreads: www.goodreads.com/LBKamps
Amazon Author Page:
www.amazon.com/author/lisabkamps
Instagram: www.instagram.com/lbkamps/
BookBub: www.bookbub.com/authors/lisa-b-kamps

CROSSING THE LINE
The Baltimore Banners Book 1

Amber "AJ" Johnson is a freelance writer who has one chance of winning her dream-job as a full-time staffer: capture an interview with the very private goalie of Baltimore's hockey team, Alec Kolchak. But he's the one man who tries her patience, even as he brings to life a quiet passion she doesn't want to admit exists.

Alec has no desire to be interviewed--he never has, never will. But he finds himself a reluctant admirer of AJ's determination to get what she wants...and he certainly never counted on his attraction to her. In a fit of frustration, he accepts AJ's bet: if she can score just one goal on him in a practice shoot-out, he would not only agree to the interview, he would let her have full access to him for a month, 24/7.

It's a bet neither one of them wants to lose...and a bet neither one can afford to win. But when it comes time to take the shot, can either one of them cross the line?

Turn the page for an exciting peek at *CROSSING THE LINE*, available now.

"Oh my God, what have I done?" AJ muttered the phrase under her breath for the hundredth time. She wanted to rub her chest but she couldn't reach it under the thick pads now covering her. She wanted to go home and curl up in a dark corner and forget about the whole thing.

Me and my bright ideas.

"Are you going to be okay?"

AJ snapped her head up and looked at Ian. The poor guy had been given the job of helping her get dressed in the pads, and she almost felt sorry for him. Almost. Between her nervousness and the threat of an impending migraine, she was too preoccupied to muster much sympathy for anyone else right now.

"Yeah, I'm fine." She took a deep breath and stood, wobbling for only a second on the skates. This was not how she had imagined the bet going. When she cooked up the stupid idea, she had figured on having a few days to at least practice.

Well, not really. If she was honest with herself, she never even imagined that Alec would agree to it. But if he had, then she would have had a few days to practice.

So much for her imagination.

She took another deep breath then followed Ian from the locker room. It didn't take too long for her gait to even out and she muttered a thankful prayer. She only hoped that she didn't sprawl face-first as soon as she stepped on the ice.

Her right hand clenched around the stick, getting used to the feel of it, getting used to the fit of the bulky glove—which was too big to begin with. This would have been so much easier if all she had to do was put on a pair of skates. She had never considered the possibility of having to put all the gear on, right down to the helmet that was a heavy weight bearing down on her head.

She really needed to do something with her imagination and its lack of thinking things all the way through.

AJ took another deep breath when they finally reached the ice. She reached out to open the door but was stopped by Ian.

"Listen, AJ, I'm not even going to pretend I know what's going on or why you think you can do this, but I'll give you some advice. Shoot fast and low, and aim for the five and two holes—those are Alec's weak spots. The five hole is—"

"Between the legs, I know." AJ winced at the sharpness of her voice. Ian was only trying to help her. He had no reason to realize she knew anything about ice hockey, and not just because she liked to write about it. She offered him a smile to take the bite from her words then slammed the butt of the stick down against the door latch so it would swing open. Two steps later and she was standing on a solid sheet of thick ice.

AJ breathed deeply several times then slowly made her way to the other side of the rink, where Alec was nonchalantly leaning against the top post of the net talking to Nathan. They both watched as she skated up to them and came to a smooth stop. Alec's face was expressionless as he studied her, and she wondered what thoughts were going through his mind. Probably nothing she really wanted to know.

Nathan nodded at her, offering a small smile. She had to give the guy some credit for not laughing in her face when she asked his opinion on her idea. "Well, at least it looks like you've been on skates before. That's a plus."

AJ didn't say anything, just absently nodded in his direction. The carefree attitude she had been aiming for was destroyed by the helmet sliding down over her forehead. She pushed it back on her head then glanced at the five pucks lined neatly on the goal line. All she had to do was get one of them across. Just one.

She didn't have a chance.

She pushed the pessimistic thought to the back of her mind. "So, do I get a chance to warm up or take a practice shot?"

Alec sized her up then briskly shook his head. "No."

AJ swallowed and glanced at the pucks, then back at Alec. "Alrighty then. A man of few words. That's what I like about you, Kolchak." AJ though he might have cracked a smile behind his mask but she couldn't be sure. She sighed and leaned on her stick, trying to look casual and hoping it didn't slip out from under her and send her sprawling. "So, what are the rules?"

"Simple. You get five chances to shoot. If you score, you win. If you don't, I win." Alec swept the pucks to the side with the blade of his stick so Nathan could pick them up. She followed the moves with her eyes and tried to ignore the pounding in her chest.

She had so much riding on this. Something told her that Alec was dead serious about being left alone if she lost. It had been a stupid idea, and she wondered if she would have had better luck at trying to wear him down the old-fashioned way.

She studied his posture and decided probably not. He had been mostly patient with her up to this point, but even she knew he would have reached his limit soon.

"All or nothing, then. Fair enough. So, are you ready?"

AJ didn't hear his response but thought it was probably something sarcastic. She sighed then turned to follow Nathan to the center line, her heart beating too fast as her feet glided across the ice. She shrugged her shoulders, trying to readjust the bulk of the pads, and watched as Nathan lined the pucks up.

He finished then straightened and faced her, an unreadable expression on his face. He finally grinned and shook his head.

"I have no idea if you know what you're doing or not, but good luck. You're going to need it."

"Gee, thanks."

Nathan walked across the ice to the bench and leaned against the outer boards, joining a few of the other players gathered there. AJ wished they were gone, that they had something better to do than stand around and watch her make a fool of herself.

Well, she had brought it on herself.

She closed her eyes and inhaled deeply, pushing everything from her mind except what she was about to do. When she opened her eyes again, her gaze was on the first puck. Heavy, solid...nothing more than a slab of black rubber...

Okay, so she wasn't going to have any luck becoming one with the puck. Stupid idea. AJ had never understood that whole Zen thing anyway.

She swallowed and began skating in small circles, testing her ankles as she turned first one way then another, testing the stick as she swept it back and forth across the ice in front of her. Not too bad. Maybe she hadn't forgotten—

"Sometime today would be nice!"

AJ winced at the sarcasm in Alec's voice and wished she had some kind of comeback for him. Instead she mumbled to herself and got into position behind the first puck. She didn't even look up to see if he was ready. Didn't ask if it was okay to start, she just pushed off hard and skated, the stick out in front of her.

This was her one shot, she couldn't blow it.

PLAYING THE GAME
The York Bombers Book 1

Harland Day knows what it's like to be on rock bottom: he was there once before, years ago when his mother walked out and left him behind. But he learned how to play the game and survived, crawling his way up with the help of a friend-turned-lover. This time is different: he has nobody to blame but himself for his trip to the bottom. His mouth, his attitude, his crappy play that landed him back in the minors instead of playing pro hockey with the Baltimore Banners. And this time, he doesn't have anyone to help him out, not when his own selfishness killed the most important relationship he ever had.

Courtney Williams' life isn't glamorous or full of fame and fortune but she doesn't need those things to be happy. She of all people knows there are more important things in life. And, for the most part, she's been able to forget what could have been--until Harland gets reassigned to the York Bombers and shows back up in town, full of attitude designed to hide the man underneath. But the arrogant hockey player can't hide from her, the one person who knows him better than anyone else. They had been friends. They had been lovers. And then they had been torn apart by misunderstanding and betrayal.

But some ties are hard to break. Can they look past what had been and move forward to what could be? Or will the sins of the past haunt them even now, all these years later?

Turn the page for a preview of PLAYING THE GAME, the launch title of The York Bombers, now available.

The third drink was still in his hand, virtually untouched. He glanced down at it, briefly wondered if he should just put it down and walk away. It was still early, not even eleven yet. Maybe if he stuck it out for another hour; maybe if he finished this drink and let the whiskey loosen him up. Or maybe if he just paid attention to the girl draped along his side—

Maybe.

He swirled the glass in his hand and brought it to his mouth, taking a long sip of mostly melted ice. The girl next to him—what the fuck was her name?—pushed her body even closer, the swell of her barely-covered breast warm against the bare flesh of his arm.

"So you're a hockey player, right? One of Zach's teammates?"

Her breath held a hint of red wine, too sweet. Harland tried not to grimace, pushed the memories at bay as his stomach lurched. He tightened his grip on the glass—if he was too busy holding something, he couldn't put his arm around her or push her away—and glanced down. The girl looked like she was barely old enough to be in this place. A sliver of fright shot through him. They did card here, right? He wasn't about to be busted picking up someone underage, was he?

She had a killer body, slim and lean with just enough muscle tone in her arms and legs to reassure him that she didn't starve herself and probably worked out. Long tanned legs that went on for miles and dainty feet shoved into shoes that had to have heels at least five inches tall. He grimaced and briefly wondered how the hell she was even standing in them.

Of course, she *was* leaning against him, her full breasts pushing against his arm and chest. Maybe that was because she couldn't stand in those ridiculous heels. Heels like that weren't meant for walking—they were fuck-me heels, meant for the bedroom.

He looked closer, at her platinum-streaked hair carefully crafted in a fuck-me style and held in place by what had to be a full can of hairspray—or whatever the fuck women used nowadays. Thick mascara coated her lashes, or maybe they weren't even her real lashes, now that he was actually looking. No, he doubted they were real. That was a shame because from what he could see, she had pretty eyes, kind of a smoky gray set off by the shimmery eyeshadow coloring her lids. Hell, maybe those eyes weren't even real, maybe they were just colored contacts.

Fuck. Wasn't anything real anymore? Wasn't anyone who they really claimed to be? And why the fuck was he even worried about it when all he had to do was nod and smile and take her by the hand and lead her out? Something told him he wouldn't even have to bother with taking her home—or in his case, to a motel. No, he was pretty sure all he had to do was show her the backseat of his Expedition and that would be it.

Her full lips turned down into a pout and Harland realized she was waiting for him to answer. Yeah, she had asked him a question. What the hell had she asked?

Oh, yeah—

"Uh, yeah. Yeah, I play hockey." He took another sip of the watery drink and glanced around the crowded club. Several of his teammates were scattered around the bar, their faces alternately lit and shadowed by the colored lights pulsing in time to the music.

Jason pulled his tongue from some girl's throat long enough to motion to the mousy barmaid for a fresh drink. His gaze caught Harland's and a wide grin split his face when he nodded.

Harland got the message loud and clear. How could he miss it, when the nod was toward the girl hanging all over him? Jason was congratulating him on hooking up, encouraging him to take the next step.

Harland took another sip and looked away. Tension ran through him, as solid and real as the hand running along his chest. He looked down again, watched as slender fingers worked their way into his shirt. Nails scraped across the bare flesh of his chest, teasing him.

Annoying him.

He put the drink on the bar and reached for her hand, his fingers closing around her wrist to stop her. The girl looked up, a frown on her face. But she didn't move her hand away. No, she kept trying to reach for him instead.

"What'd you say your name was?"

"Does it matter?" Her lips tilted up into a seductive smile, full of heated promise as her fingers wiggled against his chest.

Did it matter? It shouldn't, not when all Harland had to do was smile back and release her hand and let her continue. Or take her hand and lead her outside. So why the fuck was he hesitating? Why didn't he do just that? That was why he came here, wasn't it? To let go. Loosen up. Hook up, get things out of his system.

No. That may be why Jason and Zach and the others were here and why they brought him along—but that wasn't why he was here. So yeah, her name mattered. Maybe not to him, not in that sense. He just wanted to know she was interested in *him* and not what he did. That he wasn't just a trophy for her, a conquest to be bragged about to her friends in the morning.

He gently tightened his hand around her wrist and pulled her arm away, out of reach of his chest. "Yeah. It matters."

Something flashed in her eyes—surprise? Impatience? Hell if he knew. He watched her struggle with a frown, almost like she didn't want him to see it. Then she pasted another bright smile on her face, this one a little too forced, and pulled her arm from his grasp.

"It's Shayla." She stepped even closer, running her hand along his chest and down, her finger tracing the waistband of his jeans.

He almost didn't stop her. Temptation seized him, fisting his gut, searing his blood. It would be easy, so easy.

Too easy.

Then a memory of warm brown eyes, wide with innocence, came to mind. Clear, sharp and almost painful. Harland closed his eyes, his breath hitching in his chest as the picture in his mind grew, encompassing soft brown hair and perfect lips, curled in a trembling smile.

"Fuck." His eyes shot open. He grabbed the girl's hand—Shayla's—just as she started to stroke him through the worn denim. Her own eyes narrowed and she made no attempt to hide her frown this time.

"What are you doing?" Her voice was sharp, biting.

"I could ask you the same thing."

Her hand twisted in his grip. Once, twice. "Zach told me you needed to loosen up. That you were looking for a little fun."

Zach had put her up to this? Harland should have

known. He narrowed his eyes, not surprised when the girl suddenly stiffened. Could she see his distaste? Sense his condemnation? He leaned forward, his mouth close to her ear, his voice flat and cold.

"Maybe you want me to whip my cock out right here so you can get on your knees and suck me off? Have everyone watch? Will that do it for you?"

She ripped her hand from his grasp and pushed him away, anger coloring her face. "You're a fucking asshole."

Harland straightened and fixed her with a flat smile. "You're right. I am."

She said something else, the words too low for him to hear, then spun around and walked away. Her steps were short, angry, and he had to bite back a smile when she teetered to the side and almost fell.

Loathing filled him, leaving him cold and empty. Not loathing of the girl—no, the loathing was all directed at himself. What the fuck was his problem?

The girl was right: he was a fucking asshole. A loathsome bastard.

Harland yanked the wallet from his back pocket and pulled out several bills, enough to cover whatever he'd had to drink and then some. He tossed down the watered whiskey, barely feeling the slight burn as it worked its way down his throat. Then he turned and stormed toward the door, ignoring the sound of his name being called.

He should have gone home, back to the three-bedroom condo he was now forced to share with the sorry excuse that passed for his father. But he wasn't in the mood to deal with his father's bullshit, not in the mood to deal with anything. So he drove, with no destination in mind, needing distance.

Distance from the spectacle he had just made of himself.

Distance from what he had become.

Distance from who he was turning into.

But how in the hell was he supposed to distance himself...from himself?

Harland turned into a residential neighborhood, driving blindly, his mind on autopilot. He finally stopped, eased the SUV against the curb, and cut the engine.

Silence greeted him. Heavy, almost accusing. He rested his head against the steering wheel and squeezed his eyes shut. He didn't need to look around to know where he was, didn't need to view the quiet street filled with small houses that showed years of wear. Years of life and happiness and grief and torment.

"Fuck." The word came out in a strangled whisper and he straightened in the seat, running one hand down his face. Why did he keep coming here? Why did he keep tormenting himself?

She didn't want to see him, would probably shove him off the small porch if he ever dared to knock on the door. He knew that, as sure as he knew his own name.

As sure as he knew that she'd be sickened by what he had become. Three years had gone by. Three years where he'd never bothered to even contact her. Hell, maybe he was being generous. Maybe he was giving himself more importance than he deserved. Maybe she didn't even remember him.

He rubbed one hand across his eyes and took in a ragged breath, then turned his head to the side. The house was dark, just like almost every other house on the block. But he didn't need light to see it, not when it was so clear in his mind.

A simple cottage style home, with plain white siding that was always one season away from needing a new coat of paint. Flowerbeds filled with exploding color that hid the age of the house. A small backyard filled with more flowers and a picnic table next to the old grill, where something was always being fixed during the warmer months.

An image of each room filled his mind, one after the other, like a choppy movie playing on an old screen. Middle class, blue collar—but full of laughter and warm memories. He knew the house, better than his own.

He should. He'd spent more time here growing up than he had at his own run-down house the next street over. He had come here to escape, stayed because it was an oasis in his own personal desert of despair.

Until he had ruined even that.

He closed his eyes against the memories, shutting them out with a small whimper of pain. Then he started the truck and pulled away, trying to put distance between himself and the past.

A past that was suddenly more real than the present.